A MATTER OF JOB SECURITY

Mitch found what he was looking for on the front page of the **New York Times** . . . and he really wished he hadn't.

The first column contained the obituary of Mitchell Courtenay, head of Fowler Schocken Associates, Venus Section.

According to the story he had been found frozen to death on Starrzelius Glacier near Little America. He had evidently been tampering with his power pack, and it had failed.

A likely story!

Somebody wanted him dead, and somebody wanted it now!

But Mitch wasn't ready to die, and he was determined to live long enough to find out who was waiting for him to fall off the corporate ladder!

"As satire that not only bites but pinches and teases, The Space Merchants is wickedly skillful."
—*Publishers Weekly*

". . . one of the true classics in the field. Highly recommended!"
—*Locus*

HAIL *THE SPACE MERCHANTS*

"Messrs. Pohl and Kornbluth have taken us 250 years into the future of the advertising world—there is no other; for the hucksters have inherited the earth . . . a bitter satire on the conscience-less activities of the ad men, but the lapse of two centuries plus some very funny remarks and situations cushion the bumps enough so that the reader is merely taken for a very funny ride."

—*St. Louis Post Dispatch*

"The Space Merchants, clearly, is an admonitory satire on certain aspects of our own society, mainly economic; but it is not only that. It does not simply show the already impending consequences of the growth of industrial and commercial power, and it does more than simply satirize or criticize existing habits in the advertising profession, though to its work in this direction it adds some effective parody. Beyond all this, the book seems to be interested in the future as such, to inquire what might result from turns of events that are possible . . ."

—*Kingsley Amis*

"In The Space Merchants we have some of the best satire of our times; it has The Hucksters beat all hollow."

—*Denver Post*

Also by Frederik Pohl
Published by Ballantine Books:

The
Space Merchants

BY
FREDERIK POHL
AND
C. M. KORNBLUTH

A Del Rey Book

BALLANTINE BOOKS • NEW YORK

A Del Rey Book
Published by Ballantine Books

A condensed version of this novel appeared in GALAXY
magazine under the title *Gravy Planet*.

Library of Congress Catalog Card Number: 53-6886

ISBN 0-345-29697-4

Manufactured in the United States of America

First Edition: May 1953
Twelfth Printing: July 1981

The
Space Merchants

1

AS I DRESSED
that morning I ran over in my mind the long list of
statistics, evasions, and exaggerations that they
would expect in my report. My section—Production—had been plagued with a long series of ill-
nesses and resignations, and you can't get work
done without people to do it. But the Board
wasn't likely to take that as an excuse.

I rubbed depilatory soap over my face and
rinsed it with the trickle from the fresh-water
tap. Wasteful, of course, but I pay taxes and salt
water always leaves my face itchy. Before the last
of the greasy stubble was quite washed away the
trickle stopped and didn't start again. I swore a
little and finished rinsing with salt. It had been
happening lately; some people blamed Consie
saboteurs. Loyalty raids were being held through-
out the New York Water Supply Corporation; so
far they hadn't done any good.

The morning newscast above the shaving mirror caught me for a moment . . . the President's
speech of last night, a brief glimpse of the Venus

rocket squat and silvery on the Arizona sand, rioting in Panama . . . I switched it off when the quarter-hour time signal chimed over the audio band.

It looked as though I was going to be late again. Which certainly would not help mollify the Board.

I saved five minutes by wearing yesterday's shirt instead of studding a clean one and by leaving my breakfast juice to grow warm and sticky on the table. But I lost the five minutes again by trying to call Kathy. She didn't answer the phone and I was late getting into the office.

Fortunately — and unprecedentedly — Fowler Schocken was late too.

In our office it is Fowler's custom to hold the weekly Board conference fifteen minutes before the regular opening of the business day. It keeps the clerks and stenos on their toes, and it's no hardship to Fowler. He spends every morning in the office anyway, and "morning" to him begins with the rising of the sun.

Today, though, I had time to get my secretary's summary off my desk before the meeting. When Fowler Schocken walked in with a courteous apology for his tardiness I was sitting in my place at the foot of the table, reasonably relaxed and as sure of myself as a Fowler Schocken Associate is ever likely to be.

"Good morning," Fowler said, and the eleven of us made the usual idiot murmur. He didn't sit down; he stood gazing paternally at us for about a minute and a half. Then, with the air of a daytripper in Xanadu, he looked carefully and delightedly about the room.

"I've been thinking about our conference room," he said, and we all looked around at it. The room

2

isn't big, it isn't small: say ten by twelve. But it's cool, well-lighted, and most imposingly furnished. The air recirculators are cleverly hidden behind animated friezes; the carpeting is thick and soft; and every piece of furniture is constructed from top to bottom of authentic, expertized, genuine tree-grown wood.

Fowler Schocken said: "We have a nice conference room here, men. As we should have, since Fowler Schocken Associates is the largest advertising agency in the city. We bill a megabuck a year more than anybody else around. And—" he looked around at all of us, "I think you'll agree that we all find it worth while. I don't think there's a person in this room who has less than a two-room apartment." He twinkled at me. "Even the bachelors. Speaking for myself, I've done well. My summer place looks right over one of the largest parks on Long Island. I haven't tasted any protein but new meat for years, and when I go out for a spin I pedal a Cadillac. The wolf is a long way from my door. And I think any one of you can say the same. Right?" The hand of our Director of Market Research shot up and Fowler nodded at him: "Yes, Matthew?"

Matt Runstead knows which side his bread is oiled on. He glared belligerently around the table. "I just want to go on record as agreeing with Mr. Schocken—one hundred per cent—all the way!" he snapped.

Fowler Schocken inclined his head. "Thank you, Matthew." And he meant it. It took him a moment before he could go on. "We all know," he said, "what put us where we are. We remember the Starrzelius Verily account, and how we put Indiastries on the map. The first spherical trust.

3

Merging a whole subcontinent into a single manufacturing complex. Schocken Associates pioneered on both of them. Nobody can say we were floating with the tide. But that's behind us.

"Men! I want to know something. You can tell me truthfully—are we getting soft?" He took time to look at each of our faces searchingly, ignoring the forest of hands in the air. God help me, mine was right up there too. Then he waved to the man at his right. "You first, Ben," he said.

Ben Winston stood up and baritoned: "Speaking for Industrial Anthropology, no! Listen to today's progress report—you'll get it in the noon bulletin, but let me brief you now: according to the midnight indices, all primary schools east of the Mississippi are now using our packaging recommendation for the school lunch program. Soyaburgers and regenerated steak"—there wasn't a man around the table who didn't shudder at the thought of soyaburgers and regenerated steak— "are packed in containers the same shade of green as the Universal products. But the candy, ice cream, and Kiddiebutt cigarette ration are wrapped in colorful Starrzelius red. When those kids grow up . . ." he lifted his eyes exultantly from his notes. "According to our extrapolation, fifteen years from now Universal products will be broke, bankrupt, and off the market entirely!"

He sat down in a wave of applause. Schocken clapped too, and looked brightly at the rest of us. I leaned forward with Expression One—eagerness, intelligence, competence—all over my face. But I needn't have bothered. Fowler pointed to the lean man next to Winston. Harvey Bruner.

"I don't have to tell you men that Point-of-Sale has its special problems," Harvey said, puffing his thin cheeks. "I swear, the whole damned Government must be infiltrated with Consies! You know what they've done. They outlawed compulsive subsonics in our aural advertising—but we've bounced back with a list of semantic cue words that tie in with every basic trauma and neurosis in American life today. They listened to the safety cranks and stopped us from projecting our messages on aircar windows—but we bounced back. Lab tells me," he nodded to our Director of Research across the table, "that soon we'll be testing a system that projects direct on the retina of the eye.

"And not only that, but we're going forward. As an example I want to mention the Coffiest pro—" He broke off. "Excuse me, Mr. Schocken," he whispered. "Has Security checked this room?"

Fowler Schocken nodded. "Absolutely clean. Nothing but the usual State Department and House of Representatives spy-mikes. And of course we're feeding a canned playback into them."

Harvey relaxed again. "Well, about this Coffiest," he said. "We're sampling it in fifteen key cities. It's the usual offer—a thirteen-week supply of Coffiest, one thousand dollars in cash, and a weekend vacation on the Ligurian Riviera to everybody who comes in. But—and here's what makes this campaign truly great, in my estimation—each sample of Coffiest contains three milligrams of a simple alkaloid. Nothing harmful. But definitely habit-forming. After ten weeks the customer is hooked for life. It would cost him at least five thousand dollars for a cure, so it's simpler for him to go right on drinking Coffiest—three cups with every meal and a pot beside his bed at night, just as it says on the jar."

5

Fowler Schocken beamed, and I braced myself into Expression One again. Next to Harvey sat Tildy Mathis, Chief of Personnel and handpicked by Schocken himself. But he didn't ask women to speak at Board sessions, and next to Tildy sat me.

I was composing my opening remarks in my head as Fowler Schocken let me down with a smile. He said: "I won't ask every section to report. We haven't the time. But you've given me your answer, gentlemen. It's the answer I like. You've met every challenge up to now. And so now—I want to give you a new challenge."

He pressed a button on his monitor panel and swiveled his chair around. The lights went down in the room; the projected Picasso that hung behind Schocken's chair faded and revealed the mottled surface of the screen. On it another picture began to form.

I had seen the subject of that picture once before that day, in my news screen over my shaving mirror.

It was the Venus rocket, a thousand-foot monster, the bloated child of the slim V-2's and stubby Moon rockets of the past. Around it was a scaffolding of steel and aluminum, acrawl with tiny figures that manipulated minute, blue-white welding flames. The picture was obviously recorded; it showed the rocket as it had been weeks or months ago in an earlier stage of construction, not poised as if ready for take-off, as I had seen it earlier.

A voice from the screen said triumphantly and inaccurately: "This is the ship that spans the stars!" I recognized the voice as belonging to one of the

6

organ-toned commentators in Aural Effects and expertized the scripts without effort as emanating from one of Tildy's girl copywriters. The talented slovenliness that would confuse Venus with a star had to come from somebody on Tildy's staff.

"This is the ship that a modern Columbus will drive through the void," said the voice. "Six and a half million tons of trapped lightning and steel —an ark for eighteen hundred men and women, and everything to make a new world for their home. Who will man it? What fortunate pioneers will tear an empire from the rich, fresh soil of another world? Let me introduce you to them —a man and his wife, two of the intrepid . . ."

The voice kept on going. On the screen the picture dissolved to a spacious suburban roomette in early morning. On the screen the husband folding the bed into the wall and taking down the partition to the children's nook; the wife dialing breakfast and erecting the table. Over the breakfast juices and the children's pablum (with a steaming mug of Coffiest for each, of course) they spoke persuasively to each other about how wise and brave they had been to apply for passage in the Venus rocket. And the closing question of their youngest babbler ("Mommy, when I grow up kin I take *my* littul boys and girls to a place as nice as Venus?") cued the switch to a highly imaginative series of shots of Venus as it would be when the child grew up—verdant valleys, crystal lakes, brilliant mountain vistas.

The commentary did not exactly deny, and neither did it dwell on, the decades of hydroponics and life in hermetically sealed cabins that

7

the pioneers would have to endure while working on Venus's unbreathable atmosphere and waterless chemistry.

Instinctively I had set the timer button on my watch when the picture started. When it was over I read the dial: nine minutes! Three times as long as any commercial could legally run. One full minute more than we were accustomed to get.

It was only after the lights were on again, the cigarettes lit, and Fowler Schocken well into his pep talk for the day that I began to see how that was possible.

He began in the dithering, circumlocutory way that has become a part of the flavor of our business. He called out attention to the history of advertising—from the simple handmaiden task of selling already-manufactured goods to its present role of creating industries and redesigning a world's folkways to meet the needs of commerce. He touched once more on what we ourselves, Fowler Schocken Associates, had done with our own expansive career. And then he said:

"There's an old saying, men. 'The world is our oyster.' We've made it come true. But we've eaten that oyster." He crushed out his cigarette carefully. "We've eaten it," he repeated. "We've actually and literally conquered the world. Like Alexander, we weep for new worlds to conquer. And *there*—" he waved at the screen behind him, "*there* you have just seen the first of those worlds."

I have never liked Matt Runstead, as you may have gathered. He is a Paul Pry whom I suspect of wire tapping even within the company. He must have spied out the Venus project well in advance, because not even the most talented reflexes could have brought out his little speech.

8

While the rest of us were still busy assimilating what Fowler Schocken had told us, Runstead was leaping to his feet.

"Gentlemen," he said with passion, "this is truly the work of genius. Not just India. Not just a commodity. But a whole planet to *sell*. I salute you, Fowler Schocken—the Clive, the Bolivar, the John Jacob Astor of a new world!"

Matt was first, as I say, but every one of us got up and said in turn about the same thing. Including me. It was easy; I'd been doing it for years. Kathy had never understood it and I'd tried to explain, with the light touch, that it was a religious ritual—like the champagne-bottle smash on the ship's prow, or the sacrifice of the virgin to the corn crop. Even with the light touch I never pressed the analogy too far. I don't think any of us, except maybe Matt Runstead, would feed opium derivatives to the world for money alone. But listening to Fowler Schocken speak, hypnotizing ourselves with our antiphonal responses, made all of us capable of any act that served our god of Sales.

I do not mean to say that we were criminals. The alkaloids in Coffiest were, as Harvey pointed out, not harmful.

When all of us had done, Fowler Schocken touched another button and showed us a chart. He explained it carefully, item by item; he showed us tables and graphs and diagrams of the entire new Department of Fowler Schocken Associates which would be set up to handle development and exploitation of the planet Venus. He covered the tedious lobbying and friendmaking in Congress, which had given us the exclusive right to levy tribute and collect from the planet

—and I began to see how he could safely use a nine-minute commercial. He explained how the Government—it's odd how we still think and talk of that clearinghouse for pressures as though it were an entity with a will of its own—how the Government wanted Venus to be an American planet and how they had selected the peculiarly American talent of advertising to make it possible. As he spoke we all caught some of his fire. I envied the man who would head the Venus Section; any one of us would have been proud to take the job.

He spoke of trouble with the Senator from Du Pont Chemicals with his forty-five votes, and of an easy triumph over the Senator from Nash-Kelvinator with his six. He spoke proudly of a faked Consie demonstration against Fowler Schocken, which had lined up the fanatically anti-Consie Secretary of the Interior. Visual Aids had done a beautiful job of briefing the information, but we were there nearly an hour looking at the charts and listening to Fowler's achievements and plans.

But finally he clicked off the projector and said: "There you have it. That's our new campaign. And it starts right away—*now*. I have only one more announcement to make and then we can all get to work."

Fowler Schocken is a good showman. He took the time to find a slip of paper and read from it a sentence that the lowest of our copyboys could deliver off the cuff. "The chairman of the Venus Section," he read, "will be Mitchell Courtenay."

And that was the biggest surprise of all, because Mitchell Courtenay is me.

2

I LINGERED
with Fowler for three or four minutes while the rest
of the Board went back to their offices, and the
elevator ride down from the Board room to my
own office on the eighty-sixth floor took a few
seconds. So Hester was already clearing out my
desk when I arrived.

"Congratulations, Mr. Courtenay," she said.
"You're moving to the eighty-ninth now. Isn't it
wonderful? And I'll have a private office too!"

I thanked her and picked up the phone over
the desk. The first thing I had to do was to get
my staff in and turn over the reins of Production;
Tom Gillespie was next in line. But the first thing
I *did* was to dial Kathy's apartment again. There
was still no answer, so I called in the boys.

They were properly sorry to see me go and
properly delighted about everybody's moving up
a notch.

And then it was lunch time, so I postponed
the problem of the planet Venus until the afternoon.

11

I made a phone call, ate quickly in the company cafeteria, took the elevator down to the shuttle, and the shuttle south for sixteen blocks. Coming out, I found myself in the open air for the first time that day, and reached for my antisoot plugs but didn't put them in. It was raining lightly and the air had been a little cleared. It was summer, hot and sticky; the hordes of people crowding the sidewalks were as anxious as I to get back inside a building. I had to bulldoze my way across the street and into the lobby.

The elevator took me up fourteen floors. It was an old building with imperfect air conditioning, and I felt a chill in my damp suit. It occurred to me to use that fact instead of the story I had prepared, but I decided against it.

A girl in a starched white uniform looked up as I walked into the office. I said: "My name is Silver. Walter P. Silver. I have an appointment."

"Yes, Mr. Silver," she remembered. "Your heart —you said it was an emergency."

"That's right. Of course it's probably psychosomatic, but I felt—"

"Of course." She waved me to a chair. "Dr. Nevin will see you in just a moment."

It was ten minutes. A young woman came out of the doctor's office, and a man who had been waiting in the reception room before me went in; then he came out and the nurse said: "Will you go into Dr. Nevin's office now?"

I went in. Kathy, very trim and handsome in her doctor's smock, was putting a case chart in her desk. When she straightened up she said, "Oh, Mitch!" in a very annoyed tone.

"I told only one lie," I said. "I lied about my

name. But it is an emergency. And my heart is involved."

There was a faint impulse toward a smile, but it didn't quite reach the surface. "Not medically," she said.

"I *told* your girl it was probably psychosomatic. She said to come in anyhow."

"I'll speak to her about that. Mitch, you know I can't see you during working hours. Now please—"

I sat down next to her desk. "You won't see me any time, Kathy. What's the trouble?"

"Nothing's the trouble. Please go away, Mitch. I'm a doctor; I have work to do."

"Nothing as important as this. Kathy, I tried to call you all last night and all morning."

She lit a cigarette without looking at me. "I wasn't home," she said.

"No, you weren't." I leaned forward and took the cigarette from her and puffed on it. She hesitated, shrugged, and took out another. I said: "I don't suppose I have the right to ask my wife where she spends her time?"

Kathy flared: "Damn it, Mitch, you know—" Her phone rang. She screwed her eyes shut for a moment. Then she picked up the phone, leaning back in her chair, looking across the room, relaxed, a doctor soothing a patient. It took only a few moments. But when it was all over she was entirely self-possessed.

"Please go away," she said, stubbing out her cigarette.

"Not until you tell me when you'll see me."

"I . . . haven't time to see you, Mitch. I'm not your wife. You have no right to bother me like this. I could have you enjoined or arrested."

13

"My certificate's on file," I reminded her.

"Mine isn't. It never will be. As soon as the year is up, we're through, Mitch."

"There was something I wanted to tell you." Kathy had always been reachable through curiosity.

There was a long pause and instead of saying again: "Please go away," she said: "Well, what is it?" *she's very curious*

I said: "It's something big. It calls for a celebration. And I'm not above using it as an excuse to see you for just a little while tonight. Please, Kathy—I love you very much and I promise not to make a scene."

". . . No."

But she had hesitated. I said: "Please?"

"Well—" While she was thinking, her phone rang. "All right," she said to me. "Call me at home. Seven o'clock. Now let me take care of the sick people." *submissive in the end*

She picked up the phone. I let myself out of her office while she was talking, and she didn't look after me.

Fowler Schocken was hunched over his desk as I walked in, staring at the latest issue of *Taunton's Weekly*. The magazine was blinking in full color as the triggered molecules of its inks collected photons by driblets and released them in bursts. He waved the brilliant pages at me and asked: "What do you think of this, Mitch?"

"Sleazy advertising," I said promptly. "If we had to stoop so low as to sponsor a magazine like Taunton Associates—well, I think I'd resign. It's too cheap a trick."

"Um." He put the magazine face down; the

flashing inks gave one last burst and subsided as their light source was cut off. "Yes, it's cheap," he said thoughtfully. "But you have to give them credit for enterprise. Taunton gets sixteen and a half million readers for *his* ads every week. Nobody else's—just Taunton clients. And I hope you didn't mean that literally about resigning. I just gave Harvey the go-ahead on *Shock*. The first issue comes out in the fall, with a print order of twenty million. No—" He mercifully held up his hand to cut off my stammering try at an explanation. "I understood what you meant, Mitch. You were against *cheap* advertising. And so am I. Taunton is to me the epitome of everything that keeps advertising from finding its rightful place with the clergy, medicine, and the bar in our way of life. There isn't a shoddy trick he wouldn't pull, from bribing a judge to stealing an employee. And, Mitch, he's a man you'll have to watch."

"Why? I mean, why particularly?"

Schocken chuckled. "Because we stole Venus from him, that's why. I told you he was enterprising. He had the same idea I did. It wasn't easy to persuade the Government that it should be our baby." *stole Venus*

"I see," I said. And I did. Our representative government now is perhaps more representative than it has ever been before in history. It is not necessarily representative *per capita,* but it most surely is *ad valorem.* If you like philosophical problems, here is one for you: should each human being's vote register alike, as the lawbooks pretend and as some say the founders of our nation desired? Or should a vote be weighed according to the wisdom, the power, and the influence—that is, the money—of the voter? That is a philosophical

15

problem for you, you understand; not for me. I am a pragmatist, and a pragmatist, moreover, on the payroll of Fowler Schocken.

One thing was bothering me. "Won't Taunton be likely to take—well, direct action?"

"Oh, he'll try to steal it back," Fowler said mildly.

"That's not what I mean. You remember what happened with Antarctic Exploitation."

"I was there. A hundred and forty casualties on our side. God knows what they lost."

"And that was only one continent. Taunton takes these things pretty personally. If he started a feud for a lousy frozen continent, what will he do for a whole planet?"

Fowler said patiently, "No, Mitch. He wouldn't dare. Feuds are expensive. Besides, we're not giving him grounds—not grounds that would stand up in court. And, in the third place . . . we'd whip his tail off."

"I guess so," I said, and felt reassured. Believe me, I am a loyal employee of Fowler Schocken Associates. Ever since cadet days I have tried to live my life "for Company and for Sales." But industrial feuds, even in our profession, can be pretty messy. It was only a few decades ago that a small but effective agency in London filed a feud against the English branch of B.B.D. & O. and wiped it out to the man except for two Bartons and a single underage Osborn. And they say there are still bloodstains on the steps of the General Post Office where Western Union and American Railway Express fought it out for the mail contract.

Schocken was speaking again. "There's one thing you'll have to watch out for: the lunatic fringe. This is the kind of project that's bound to bring them out. Every crackpot organization on the list, from the Consies to the G.O.P., is going to come out for or against it. Make sure they're all for; they swing weight."

"Even the Consies?" I squeaked.

"Well, no. I didn't mean that; they'd be more of a liability." His white hair glinted as he nodded thoughtfully. "Mm. Maybe you could spread the word that spaceflight and Conservationism are diametrically opposed. It uses up too many raw materials, hurts the living standard—you know. Bring in the fact that the fuel uses organic material that the Consies think should be made into fertilizer—"

I like to watch an expert at work. Fowler Schocken laid down a whole subcampaign for me right there; all I had to do was fill in the details. The Conversationists were fair game, those wild-eyed zealots who pretended modern civilization was in some way "plundering" our planet. Preposterous stuff. Science is *always* a step ahead of the failure of natural resources. After all, when real meat got scarce, we had soyaburgers ready. When oil ran low, technology developed the pedicab.

I had been exposed to Consie sentiment in my time, and the arguments had all come down to one thing: Nature's way of living was the *right* way of living. Silly. If "Nature" had intended us to eat fresh vegetables, it wouldn't have given us niacin or ascorbic acid.

I sat still for twenty minutes more of Fowler Schocken's inspirational talk, and came away with the discovery I had often made before; briefly and effectively, he had given me every fact and instruction I needed.

17

The details he left to me, but I knew my job:

We wanted Venus colonized by Americans. To accomplish this, three things were needed: colonists; a way of getting them to Venus; and something for them to do when they got there.

The first was easy to handle through direct advertising. Schocken's TV commercial was the perfect model on which we could base the rest of that facet of our appeal. It is always easy to persuade a consumer that the grass is greener far away. I had already penciled in a tentative campaign with the budget well under a megabuck. More would have been extravagant.

The second was only partly our problem. The ships had been designed—by Republic Aviation, Bell Telephone Labs and U. S. Steel, I believe, under Defense Department contract. Our job wasn't to make the transportation to Venus possible but to make it palatable. When your wife found her burned-out toaster impossible to replace because its nichrome element was part of a Venus rocket's main drive jet, or when the inevitable disgruntled congressman for a small and frozen-out firm waved an appropriations sheet around his head and talked about government waste on wildcat schemes, our job began: we had to convince your wife that rockets are more important than toasters; we had to convince the congressman's constituent firm that its tactics were unpopular and would cost it profits.

I thought briefly of an austerity campaign and vetoed it. Our other accounts would suffer. A religious movement, perhaps—something that would offer vicarious dedication to the eight hundred million who would not ride the rockets themselves. . . .

18

I tabled that; Bruner could help me there. And I went on to point three. There had to be something to keep the colonists busy on Venus.

This, I knew, was what Fowler Schocken had his eye on. The government money that would pay for the basic campaign was a nice addition to our year's billing, but Fowler Schocken was too big for one-shot accounts. What we wanted was the year-after-year reliability of a major industrial complex; what we wanted was the colonists, and their children, added to our complex of accounts. Fowler, of course, hoped to repeat on an enormously magnified scale our smashing success with Indiastries. His Boards and he had organized all of India into a single giant cartel, with every last woven basket and iridium ingot and caddy of opium it produced sold through Fowler Schocken advertising. Now he could do the same with Venus. Potentially this was worth as much as every dollar of value in existence put together! A whole new planet, the size of Earth, in prospect as rich as Earth—and every micron, every milligram of it ours.

I looked at my watch. About four; my date with Kathy was for seven. I just barely had time. I dialed Hester and had her get me space on the Washington jet while I put through a call to the name Fowler had given me. The name was Jack O'Shea; he was the only human being who had been to Venus—so far. His voice was young and cocky as he made a date to see me.

We were five extra minutes in the landing pattern over Washington, and then there was a hassle at the ramp. Brink's Express guards were swarming around our plane, and their lieutenant de-

19

manded identification from each emerging passenger. When it was my turn I asked what was going on. He looked at my low-number Social Security card thoughtfully and then saluted. "Sorry to bother you, Mr. Courtenay," he apologized. "It's the Consie bombing near Topeka. We got a tip that the man might be aboard the 4:05 New York jet. Seems to have been a lemon."

"What Consie bombing was this?"

"Du Pont Raw Materials Division—we're under contract for their plant protection, you know— was opening up a new coal vein under some cornland they own out there. They made a nice little ceremony of it, and just as the hydraulic mining machine started ramming through the topsoil somebody tossed a bomb from the crowd. Killed the machine operator, his helper, and a vice-president. Man slipped away in the crowd, but he was identified. We'll get him one of these days."

"Good luck, Lieutenant," I said, and hurried on to the jetport's main rerfeshment lounge. O'Shea was waiting in a window seat, visibly annoyed, but he grinned when I apologized.

"It could happen to anybody," he said, and swinging his short legs shrilled at a waiter. When we had placed our orders he leaned back and said: "Well?"

I looked down at him across the table and looked away through the window. Off to the south the gigantic pylon of the F.D.R. memorial blinked its marker signal; behind it lay the tiny, dulled dome of the old Capitol. I, a glib ad man, hardly knew where to start. And O'Shea was enjoying it. "Well?" he asked again, amusedly, and I knew he meant: "Now all of *you* have to come to *me*, and how do you like it for a change?"

20

I took the plunge. "What's on Venus?" I asked.

"Sand and smoke," he said promptly. "Didn't you read my report?"

"Certainly. I want to know more."

"Everything's in the report. Good Lord, they kept me in the interrogation room for three solid days when I got back. If I left anything out, it's gone permanently."

I said: "That's not what I mean, Jack. Who wants to spend his life reading reports? I have fifteen men in Research doing nothing but digesting reports for me so I don't have to read them. I want to know something more. I want to get the feel of the planet. There's only one place I can get it because only one man's been there."

"And sometimes I wish I hadn't," O'Shea said wearily. "Well, where do I start? You know how they picked me—the only midget in the world with a pilot's license. And you know all about the ship. And you saw the assay reports on the samples I brought back. Not that they mean much. I only touched down once, and five miles away the geology might be entirely different."

"I know all that. Look, Jack, put it this way. Suppose you wanted a lot of people to go to Venus. What would you tell them about it?"

He laughed. "I'd tell them a lot of damn big lies. Start from scratch, won't you? What's the deal?"

I gave him a fill-in on what Schocken Associates was up to, while his round little eyes stared at me from his round little face. There is an opaque quality, like porcelain, to the features of midgets: as though the destiny that had made them small at the same time made them more perfect and polished than ordinary men, to show that their

21

lack of size did not mean lack of completion. He sipped his drink and I gulped mine between paragraphs.

When my pitch was finished I still didn't know whether he was on my side or not, and with him it mattered. He was no civil service puppet dancing to the strings that Fowler Schocken knew ways of pulling. Neither was he a civilian who could be bought with a tiny decimal of our appropriation. Fowler had helped him a little to capitalize on his fame via testimonials, books, and lectures, so he owed us a little gratitude and no more.

He said: "I wish I could help," and that made things easier.

"You can," I told him. "That's what I'm here for. Tell me what Venus has to offer."

"Damn little," he said, with a small frown chiseling across his lacquered forehead. "Where shall I start? Do I have to tell you about the atmosphere? There's free formaldehyde, you know—embalming fluid. Or the heat? It averages above the boiling point of water—if there were any water on Venus, which there isn't. Not accessible, anyhow. Or the winds? I clocked five hundred miles an hour."

"No, not exactly that," I said. "I know about that. And honestly, Jack, there are answers for all those things. I want to get the feel of the place, what you thought when you were there, how you reacted. Just start talking. I'll tell you when I've had what I wanted."

He dented his rose-marble lip with his lower teeth. "Well," he said, "let's start at the beginning. Get us another drink, won't you?"

The waiter came, took our order, and came

back with the liquor. Jack drummed on the table, sipped his rhinewine and seltzer, and began to talk.

He started way back, which was good. I wanted to know the soul of the fact, the elusive, subjective mood that underlay his technical reports on the planet Venus, the basic feeling that would put compulsion and conviction into the project.

He told me about his father, the six-foot chemical engineer, and his mother, the plump, billowy housewife. He made me feel their dismay and their ungrudging love for their thirty-five-inch son. He had been eleven years old when the subject of his adult life and work first came up. He remembered the unhappiness on their faces at his first, inevitable, offhand suggestion about the circus. It was no minor tribute to them that the subject never came up again. It was a major tribute that Jack's settled desire to learn enough engineering and rocketry to be a test pilot had been granted, paid for, and carried out in the face of every obstacle of ridicule and refusal from the schools.

Of course Venus had made it all pay off.

The Venus rocket designers had run into one major complication. It had been easy enough to get a rocket to the moon a quarter-million miles away; theoretically it was not much harder to blast one across space to the nearest other world, Venus. The question was one of orbits and time, of controlling the ship and bringing it back again. A dilemma. They could blast the ship to Venus in a few days—at so squandersome a fuel expenditure that ten ships couldn't carry it. Or they could ease it to Venus along its natural orbits as you might float a barge down a gentle river—

23

which saved the fuel but lengthened the trip to months. A man in eighty days eats twice his own weight in food, breathes nine times his weight of air, and drinks water enough to float a yawl. Did somebody say: distill water from the waste products and recirculate it; do the same with food; do the same with air? Sorry. The necessary equipment for such cycling weighs more than the food, air, and water. So the human pilot was out, obviously.

A team of designers went to work on an automatic pilot. When it was done it worked pretty well. And weighed four and one half tons in spite of printed circuits and relays constructed under a microscope.

The project stopped right there until somebody thought of that most perfect servo-mechanism: a sixty-pound midget. A third of a man in weight, Jack O'Shea ate a third of the food, breathed a third of the oxygen. With minimum-weight, low-efficiency water- and air-purifiers, Jack came in just under the limit and thereby won himself undying fame.

He said broodingly, a little drunk from the impact of two weak drinks on his small frame: "They put me into the rocket like a finger into a glove. I guess you know what the ship looked like. But did you know they *zipped* me into the pilot's seat? It wasn't a chair, you know. It was more like a diver's suit; the only air on the ship was in that suit; the only water came in through a tube to my lips. Saved weight . . ."

And the next eighty days were in that suit. It fed him, gave him water, sopped his perspiration out of its air, removed his body wastes. If necessary it would have shot novocaine into a broken

24

arm, tourniqueted a cut femoral artery, or pumped air for a torn lung. It was a placenta, and a hideously uncomfortable one.

In the suit thirty-three days going, forty-one coming back. The six days in between were the justification for the trip.

Jack had fought his ship down through absolute blindness: clouds of gas that closed his own eyes and confused the radar, down to the skin of an unknown world. He had been within a thousand feet of the ground before he could see anything but swirling yellow. And then he landed and cut the rockets.

"Well, I couldn't get out, of course," he said. "For forty or fifty reasons, somebody else will have to be the first man to set foot on Venus. Somebody who doesn't care much about breathing, I guess. Anyway, there I was, looking at it." He shrugged his shoulders, looked baffled, and said a dirty word softly. "I've told it a dozen times at lectures, but I've never got it over. I tell 'em the closest thing to it on Earth is the Painted Desert. Maybe it is; I haven't been there.

"The wind blows *hard* on Venus and it tears up the rocks. Soft rocks blow away and make the dust storms. The hard parts—well, they stick out in funny shapes and colors. Great big monument things, some of them. And the most jagged hills and crevasses you can imagine. It's something like the inside of a cave, sort of—only not dark. But the light is—funny. Nobody ever saw light like that on Earth. Orangy-brownish light, brilliant, *very* brilliant, but sort of threatening. Like the way the sky is threatening in the summer around sunset just before a smasher of a thunderstorm. Only there never is any thunderstorm because

plenty of weather

there isn't a drop of water around." He hesitated. "There is lightning. Plenty of it, but never any rain . . . I don't know, Mitch," he said abruptly. "Am I being any help to you at all?"

I took my time answering. I looked at my watch and saw that the return jet was about to leave, so I bent down and turned off the recorder in my briefcase. "You're being lots of help, Jack," I said. "But I'll need more. And I have to go now. Look, can you come up to New York and work with me for a while? I've got everything you said on tape, but I want visual stuff too. Our artists can work from the pix you brought back, but there must be more. And you're a lot more use than the photographs for what we need." I didn't mention that the artists would be drawing impressions of what Venus *would* look like if it were different from what it was. "How about it?"

Jack leaned back and looked cherubic but, though he made me sweat through a brief recap of the extensive plans his lecture agent had made for the next few weeks, he finally agreed. The Shriners' talk could be canceled, he decided, and the appointments with his ghost writers could be kept as well in New York as in Washington. We made a date for the following day just as the PA system announced that my flight was ready.

"I'll walk you to the plane," Jack offered. He slipped down from the chair and threw a bill on the table for the waiter. We walked together through the narrow aisles of the bar out into the field. Jack grinned and strutted a little at some ohs and ahs that went up as he was recognized. The field was almost dark, and the glow of Washington back-lighted the silhouettes of hovering aircraft. Drifting toward us from the freight terminal was a huge cargo 'copter, a fifty-tonner, its cargo nacelle gleaming in colors as it reflected the lights below. It was no more than fifty feet in the air, and I had to clutch my hat against the downdraft from its whirling vanes.

"Damn-fool bus drivers," Jack grunted, staring up at the 'copter. "They ought to put those things on G.C.A. Just because they're maneuverable those fan-jockeys think they can take them anywhere. If I handled a jet the way they— *Run! Run!*" Suddenly he was yelling at me and push-at my middle with both his small hands. I goggled at him; it was too sudden and disconnected to make any kind of sense. He lurched at me in a miniature body block and sent me staggering a few steps.

"What the hell—?" I started to complain, but I didn't hear my own words. They were drowned out by a mechanical snapping sound and a flutter in the beat of the rotors and then the loudest crash I had ever heard as the cargo pod of the 'copter hit the concrete a yard from where we stood. It ruptured and spilled cartons of Starrzelius Verily rolled oats. One of the crimson cylinders rolled to my toes and I stupidly picked it up and looked at it.

Overhead the lightened 'copter fluttered up and away, but I didn't see it go.

"For God's sake, get it off them!" Jack was yelling, tugging at me. We had not been alone on the field. From under the buckled aluminum reached an arm holding a briefcase, and through the compound noises in my ears I could hear a bubbling sound of human pain. That was what he meant. Get it off them. I let him pull me to the

27

tangled metal, and we tried to heave it. I got a scratched hand and tore my jacket, and then the airport people got there and brusquely ordered us away.

I don't remember walking there, but by and by I found that I was sitting on someone's suitcase, back against the wall of the terminal, with Jack O'Shea talking excitedly to me. He was cursing the class of cargo 'copter pilots and blackguarding me for standing there like a fool when he'd seen the nacelle clamps opening, and a great deal more that I didn't get. I remember his knocking the red box of breakfast food from my hand impatiently. The psychologists say I am not unusually sensitive or timorous, but I was in a state of shock that lasted until Jack was loading me into my plane.

Later on the hostess told me five people had been caught under the nacelle, and the whole affair seemed to come into focus. But not until we were halfway back to New York. At the time all I remembered, all that seemed important, was Jack's saying over and over, bitterness and anger written on his porcelain face: "Too damn many people, Mitch. Too damn much crowding. I'm with you every inch of the way. We *need* Venus, Mitch, we need the space . . ."

need
space

28

3

ment, way downtown in Bensonhurst, was not
large but it was comfortable. In a homey, sensible
way it was beautifully furnished. As who should
know better than I? I pressed the button over
the label "Dr. Nevin," and smiled at her as she
opened the door.

She did not smile back. She said two things:
"You're late, Mitch," and, "I thought you were
going to call first."

I walked in and sat down. "I was late because
I almost got killed and I didn't call because I was
late. Does that square us?" She asked the question I wanted her to ask, and I told her how close
I had come to death that evening.

Kathy is a beautiful woman with a warm,
friendly face, her hair always immaculately done
in two tones of blond, her eyes usually smiling.
I have spent a great deal of time looking at her,
but I never watched more attentively than when
I told her about the cargo nacelle near-miss. It
was, on the whole, disappointing. She was really

29

concerned for me, beyond doubt. But Kathy's heart opens to a hundred people and I saw nothing in her face to make me feel that she cared more for me than anyone else she had known for years.

So I told her my other big news, the Venus account and my stewardship of it. It was more successful; she was startled and excited and happy, and kissed me in a flurry of good feeling. But when *I* kissed *her*, as I'd been wanting to do for months, she drew away and went to sit on the other side of the room, ostensibly to dial a drink.

"You rate a toast, Mitch," she smiled. "Champagne at the least. Dear Mitch, it's *wonderful* news!"

I seized the chance. "Will you help me celebrate? Really celebrate?"

Her brown eyes were wary. "Um," she said. Then: "Sure I will, Mitch. We'll do the town together—my treat and no arguments about it. The only thing is, I'll have to leave you punctually at 2400. I'm spending the night in the hospital. I've a hysterectomy to do in the morning and I mustn't get to sleep too late. Or too drunk, either."

But she smiled.

Once again I decided not to push my luck too far. "Great," I said, and I wasn't faking. Kathy is a wonderful girl to do the town with. "Let me use your phone?"

By the time we had our drinks I had arranged for tickets to a show, a dinner table, and a reservation for a nightcap afterwards. Kathy looked a little dubious. "It's a pretty crowded program for five hours, Mitch," she said. "My hysterectomy isn't going to like it if my hand shakes." But I talked her out of it. Kathy is more resilient than that. Once she did a complete trepan the morning after we'd spent the entire night screaming out our tempers at each other, and it had gone perfectly.

The dinner, for me, was a failure. I don't pretend to be an epicure who can't stand anything but new protein. I definitely am, however, a guy who gets sore when he pays new-protein prices and gets regenerated-protein merchandise. The texture of the shashlik we both ordered was all right, but you can't hide the taste. I scratched the restaurant off my list then and there, and apologized to Kathy for it. But she laughed it off, and the show afterwards was fine. Hypnotics often give me a headache, but I slipped right into the trance state this time as soon as the film began and was none the worse for it afterwards.

The night club was packed, and the headwaiter had made a mistake in the time for our reservations. We had to wait five minutes in the anteroom, and Kathy shook her head very decisively when I pleaded for an extension on the curfew. But when the headwaiter showed us with the fanciest apologies and bows to our places at the bar and our drinks came, she leaned over and kissed me again. I felt just fine.

"Thanks," she said. "That was a wonderful evening, Mitch. Get promoted often, please. I like it."

I lit a cigarette for her and one for myself, and opened my mouth to say something. I stopped.

Kathy said, "Go ahead, say it."

"Well, I was going to say that we always have fun together."

31

"I know you were. And I was going to say that I knew what you were leading up to and that the answer still was no."

"I know you were," I said glumly. "Let's get to hell out of here."

She paid the tab and we left, inserting our antisoot plugs as we hit the street. "Cab, sir?" asked the doorman.

"Yes, please," Kathy answered. "A tandem."

He whistled up a two-man pedicab, and Kathy gave the lead boy the hospital's address. "You can come if you like, Mitch," she said, and I climbed in beside her. The doorman gave us a starting push and the cabbies grunted getting up momentum.

Unasked, I put down the top. For a moment it was like our courtship again: the friendly dark, the slight, musty smell of the canvas top, the squeak of the springs. But for a moment only. "Watch that, Mitch," she said warningly.

"Please, Kathy," I said carefully. "Let me say it anyhow. It won't take long." She didn't say no. "We were married eight months ago—all right," I said quickly as she started to speak, "it wasn't an absolute marriage. But we took the interlocutory vows. Do you remember why we did that?"

She said patiently after a moment: "We were in love."

"That's right," I said. "I loved you and you loved me. And we both had our work to think about, and we knew that sometimes it made us a little hard to get along with. So we made it interim. It had a year to run before we had to decide whether to make it permanent." I touched her hand and she didn't move it away. "Kathy dear, don't you think we knew what we were doing then? Can't we—at least—give it the year's trial? There are still four months to go. Let's try it. If the year ends and you don't want to file your certificate—well, at least I won't be able to say you didn't give me a chance. As for me, I don't have to wait. My certificate's on file now and I won't change."

We passed a street light and I saw her lips twisted into an expression I couldn't quite read. "Oh, damn it all, Mitch," she said unhappily, "I *know* you won't change. That's what makes it all so terrible. Must I sit here and call you names to convince you that it's hopeless? Do I have to tell you that you're an ill-tempered, contriving Machiavellian, selfish pig of a man to live with? I used to think you were a sweet guy, Mitch. An idealist who cared for principles and ethics instead of money. I had every reason to think so. You told me so yourself, very convincingly. You were very plausible about my work too. You boned up on medicine, you came to watch me operate three times a week, you told all our friends while I was sitting right in the room listening to you how proud you were to be married to a surgeon. It took me three months to find out what you meant by that. Anybody could marry a girl who'd be a housewife. But it took a Mitchell Courtenay to marry a first-class rated surgeon and *make* her a housewife." Her voice was tremulous. "I couldn't take it, Mitch. I never will be able to. Not the arguments, the sulkiness, and the ever-and-ever fighting. I'm a doctor. Sometimes a life depends on me. If I'm all torn up inside from battling with my husband, that life isn't safe, Mitch. Can't you see that?"

Something that sounded like a sob.

33

I asked quietly: "Kathy, don't you still love me?"

She was absolutely quiet for a long moment. Then she laughed wildly and very briefly. "Here's the hospital, Mitch," she said. "It's midnight."

I threw back the top and we climbed out. "Wait," I said to the lead boy, and walked with her to the door. She wouldn't kiss me good night and she wouldn't make a date to see me again. I stood in the lobby for twenty minutes to make sure she was really staying there that night, and then got into the cab to go to the nearest shuttle station. I was in a vile mood. It wasn't helped any when the lead boy asked innocently after I had paid him off: "Say, mister, what does Mac—Machiavellian mean?"

"Spanish for 'mind your own God-damned business,' " I told him evenly. On the shuttle I wondered sourly how rich I'd have to be before I could buy privacy.

My temper was no better when I arrived at the office next morning. It took all Hester's tact to keep me from biting her head off in the first few minutes, and it was by the grace of God that there was not a Board meeting. After I'd got my mail and the overnight accumulation of interoffice memos, Hester intelligently disappeared for a while. When she came back she brought me a cup of coffee—authentic, plantation-grown coffee. "The matron in the ladies' room brews it on the sly," she explained. "Usually she won't let us take it out because she's afraid of the Coffiest team. But now that you're star class—"

I thanked her and gave her Jack O'Shea's tape to put through channels. Then I went to work.

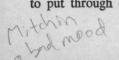
Mitch in a bad mood

First came the matter of the sampling area, and a headache with Matt Runstead. He's Market Research, and I had to work with and through him. But he didn't show any inclination to work with me. I put a map of southern California in the projector, while Matt and two of his faceless helpers boredly sprinkled cigarette ashes on my floor.

With the pointer I outlined the test areas and controls: "San Diego through Tijuana; half the communities around L.A. and the lower tip of Monterrey. Those will be controls. The rest of Cal-Mexico from L.A. down we'll use for tests. You'll have to be on the scene, I guess, Matt; I'd recommend our Diego offices as headquarters. Turner's in charge there and he's a good man."

Runstead grunted. "Not a flake of snow from year's end to year's end. Couldn't sell an overcoat there if you threw in a slave girl as a premium. For God's sake, man, why don't you leave market research to somebody who knows something about it? Don't you see how climate nulls your sigma?"

The younger of his stamped-out-of-tin assistants started to back the boss up, but I cut him off. Runstead had to be consulted on test areas—it was his job. But Venus was my project and I was going to run it. I said, sounding just a little nasty: "Regional and world income, age, density of population, health, psyche-friction, age-group distribution and mortality causes and rates are seven-place sigmas, Matt. Cal-Mex was designed personally by God Himself as a perfect testing area. In a tiny universe of less than a hundred million it duplicates every important segment of North America. I will not change my project and we are going to stick to the area I indicated." I bore down on the word "my."

Matt said : "It won't work. The temperature is the major factor. Anybody should be able to see that."

very powerful "I'm not just anybody, Matt. I'm the guy in charge."

Matt Runstead stubbed out his cigarette and got up. "Let's go talk to Fowler," he said and walked out. There wasn't anything for me to do except follow him. As I left I heard the older of his helpers picking up the phone to notify Fowler Schocken's secretary that we were coming. He had a team all right, that Runstead. I spent a little time wondering how I could build a team like that myself before I got down to the business of planning how to put it to Fowler.

But Fowler Schocken has a sure-fire technique of handling interstaff hassles. He worked it on us. When we came in he said exuberantly: "There you are! The two men I want to see! Matt, can you put out a fire for me? It's the A.I.G. people. They claim our handling of the PregNot account is hurting their trade. They're talking about going over to Taunton unless we drop PregNot. Their billing isn't much, but a birdie told me that Taunton put the idea into their heads." He went on to explain the intricacies of our relationship with the American Institute of Gynecologists. I listened only half-heartedly; our "Babies Without Maybes" campaign on their sex-determination project had given them at least a 20 per cent plus on the normal birthrate. They should be solidly ours after that. Runstead thought so too.

He said: "They don't have a case, Fowler. We sell liquor and hang-over remedies both. They've

36

got no business bitching about any other account. Besides, what the hell does this have to do with Market Research?"

Fowler chuckled happily. "That's it!" he crowed. "We throw them a switch. They'll expect the account executives to give them the usual line—but instead we'll let you handle them yourself. Snow them under with a whole line of charts and statistics to prove that PregNot never *prevents* a couple from having a baby; it just permits them to *postpone* it until they can afford to do the job right. In other words, their unit of sale goes up and their volume stays the same. And—it'll be one in the eye for Taunton. And— lawyers get disbarred for representing conflicting interests. It's cost a lot of them a lot of money. We've got to make sure that any attempt to foist the same principle on our profession is nipped in the bud. Think you can handle it for the old man, Matt?"

"Oh, hell, sure," Runstead grumbled. "What about Venus?"

Fowler twinkled at me. "What about it? Can you spare Matt for a while?"

"Forever," I said. "In fact, that's what I came to see you about. Matt's scared of southern California."

Runstead dropped his cigarette and let it lay, crisping the nylon pile of Fowler's rug. "What the hell—" he started belligerently.

"Easy," said Fowler. "Let's hear the story, Matt."

Runstead glowered at me. "All I said was that southern California isn't the right test area. What's the big difference between Venus and here? Heat! We need a test area with continental-average climate. A New Englander might be attracted by the heat on Venus; a Tijuana man, never. It's too damn hot in Cal-Mex already."

"Um," said Fowler Schocken. "Tell you what, Matt. This needs going into, and you'll want to get busy on the A.I.G. thing. Pick out a good man to vice you on the Venus section while you're out, and we'll have it hashed over at the section meeting tomorrow afternoon. Meanwhile—" he glanced at his desk clock. "Senator Danton has been waiting for seven minutes. All right?"

It was clearly not all right with Matt, and I felt cheered for the rest of the day. Things went well enough. Development came in with a report on what they'd gleaned from O'Shea's tape and all the other available material. The prospects for manufacture were there. Quick, temporary ones like little souvenir globes of Venus manufactured from the organics floating around in what we laughingly call the "air" of Venus. Long-term ones—an assay had indicated pure iron: not nine-nines pure and not ninety-nine nines pure, but absolute iron that nobody would ever find or make on an oxygen planet like Earth. The labs would pay well for it. And Development had not developed but found a remarkable little thing called a high-speed Hilsch Tube. Using no power, it could refrigerate the pioneers' homes by using the hot tornadoes of Venus. It was a simple thing that had been lying around since 1943. Nobody until us had any use for it because nobody until us had that kind of winds to play with.

Tracy Collier, the Development liaison man with Venus Section, tried also to tell me about nitrogen-fixing catalysts. I nodded from time to time and gathered that sponge-platinum "sown" on Venus would, in conjunction with the continuous, terrific lightning cause it to "snow" nitrates and "rain" hydrocarbons, purging the atmosphere of formaldehyde and ammonia.

"Kind of expensive?" I asked cautiously.

"Just as expensive as you want it to be," he said. "The platinum doesn't get used up, you know. Use one gram and take a million years or more. Use more platinum and take less time."

I didn't really understand, but obviously it was good news. I patted him and sent him on his way.

Industrial Anthropology gave me a setback. Ben Winston complained: "You *can't* make people want to live in a steam-heated sardine can. All our folkways are against it. Who's going to travel sixty million miles for a chance to spend the rest of his life cooped up in a tin shack—when he can stay right here on Earth and have corridors, elevators, streets, roofs, all the wide-open space a man could want? It's against human nature, Mitch!"

I reasoned with him. It didn't do much good. He went on telling me about the American way of life—walked to the window with me and pointed out at the hundreds of acres of rooftops where men and women could walk around in the open air, wearing simple soot-extractor nostril plugs instead of a bulky oxygen helmet.

Finally I got mad. I said: "*Somebody* must want to go to Venus. Otherwise why would they buy Jack O'Shea's book the way they do? Why would the voters stand still for a billion-and-up appropriation to build the rocket? God knows I shouldn't have to lead you by the nose this way, but here's what you are going to do: survey the bookbuyers, the repeat-viewers of O'Shea's TV shows, the ones who come early to his lectures and stand around talking in the lobby afterwards. O'Shea is on the payroll—pump him for everything you can get. Find out about the Moon colony—find out what types they have there. And then we'll know whom to aim our ads at. Any arguments, for God's sake?" There weren't.

Hester had done wonders of scheduling that first day, and I made progress with every section head involved. But she couldn't read my paper work for me, and by quitting time I had six inches of it stacked by my right arm. Hester volunteered to stay with me, but there wasn't really anything for her to do. I let her bring me sandwiches and another cup of coffee, and chased her home.

It was after eleven by the time I was done. I stopped off in an all-night diner on the fifteenth floor before heading home, a windowless box of a place where the coffee smelled of the yeast it was made from and the ham in my sandwich bore the taint of soy. But it was only a minor annoyance and quickly out of my mind. For as I opened the door to my apartment there was a *snick* and an explosion, and something slammed into the doorframe by my head. I ducked and yelled. Outside the window a figure dangling from a rope ladder drifted away, a gun in its hand.

I was stupid enough to run over to the window and gawk out at the helicopter-borne figure. I would have been a perfect target if it had been steady enough to shoot at me again, but it wasn't.

Surprised at my calm, I called the Metropolitan Protection Corporation.

"Are you a subscriber, sir?" their operator asked.

40

"Yes, dammit. For six years. Get a man over here! Get a squad over here."

"One moment, Mr. Courtenay. . . . Mr. *Mitchell* Courtenay? Copysmith, star class?"

"No," I said bitterly. "Target is my profession. Will you kindly get a man over here before the character who just took a shot at me comes back?"

"Excuse me, Mr. Courtenay," said the sweet, unruffled voice. "Did you say you were *not* a copysmith, star class?"

I ground my teeth. "I'm star class," I admitted.

"Thank you, sir. I have your record before me, sir. I am sorry, sir, but your account is in arrears. We do not accept star-class accounts at the general rate because of the risk of industrial feuds, sir." She named a figure that made each separate hair on my head stand on end.

I didn't blow my top; she was just a tool. "Thanks," I said heavily, and rang off. I put the *Program-Printing to Quarry Machinery* reel of the Red Book into the reader and spun it to Protective Agencies. I got turndowns from three or four, but finally one sleepy-sounding private detective agreed to come on over for a stiff fee.

He showed up in half an hour and I paid him, and all he did was annoy me with unanswerable questions and look for nonexistent fingerprints. After a while he went away saying he'd work on it.

I went to bed and eventually to sleep with one of the unanswered questions chasing itself around and around in my head: who would want to shoot a simple, harmless advertising man like me?

41

4

I TOOK MY
courage in my hands and walked briskly down the
hall to Fowler Schocken's office. I needed an answer, and he might have it. He might also throw
me out of the office for asking. But I needed an
answer.

It didn't seem to be the best possible time to
ask Fowler questions. Ahead of me, his door
opened explosively and Tildy Mathis lurched out.
Her face was working with emotion. She stared
at me, but I'll take oath she didn't know my
name. "Rewrites," she said wildly. "I slave my
heart out for that white-haired old rat, and what
does he give me? Rewrites. 'This is *good* copy,
but I want better than good copy from *you*,' he
says. 'Rewrite it,' he says. 'I want color,' he says,
'I want drive and beauty, and humble, human
warmth, and ecstasy, and all the tender, sad emotion of your sweet womanly heart,' he says, 'and I
want it in fifteen words.' I'll give him fifteen
words," she sobbed, and pushed past me down
the hall. "I'll give that sanctimonious, mellifluous,

hyperbolic, paternalistic, star-making, genius-devouring Moloch of an old—"

The slam of Tildy's own door cut off the noun. I was sorry; it would have been a good noun.

I cleared my throat, knocked once, and walked into Fowler's office. There was no hint of his brush with Tildy in the smile he gave me. In fact, his pink, clear-eyed face belied my suspicions, but—I *had* been shot at.

"I'll only be a minute, Fowler," I said. "I want to know whether you've been playing rough with Taunton Associates."

"I always play rough," he twinkled. "Rough, but clean."

"I mean very, very rough and very, very dirty. Have you, by any chance, tried to have any of their people shot?"

"Mitch! *Really!*"

"I'm asking," I went on doggedly, "because last night a 'copter-borne marksman tried to plug me when I came home. I can't think of any angle except retaliation from Taunton."

"Scratch Taunton," he said positively.

I took a deep breath. "Fowler," I said, "man-to-man, you haven't been Notified? I may be out of line, but I've got to ask. It isn't just me. It's the Venus Project."

There were no apples in Fowler's cheeks at that moment, and I could see in his eyes that my job and my star-class rating hung in the balance.

He said: "Mitch, I made you star class because I thought you could handle the responsibilities that came with it. It isn't just the work. I know you can do that. I thought you could live up to the commercial code as well."

I hung on. "Yes, sir," I said.

43

He sat down and lit a Starr. After just exactly the right split second of hesitation, he pushed the pack to me. "Mitch, you're a youngster, only star class a short time. But you've got power. Five words from you, and in a matter of weeks or months half a million consumers will find their lives completely changed. That's power, Mitch, absolute power. And you know the old saying. Power ennobles. Absolute power ennobles absolutely."

"Yes, sir," I said. I knew all the old sayings. I also knew that he was going to answer my question eventually.

"Ah, Mitch," he said dreamily, waving his cigarette, "we have our prerogatives and our duties and our particular hazards. You can't have one without the others. If we didn't have feuds, the whole system of checks and balances would be thrown out of gear."

"Fowler," I said, greatly daring, "you know I have no complaints about the system. It works; that's all you have to say for it. I know we need feuds. And it stands to reason that if Taunton files a feud against us, you've got to live up to the code. You can't broadcast the information; every executive in the shop would be diving for cover instead of getting work done. But—Venus Project is in my head, Fowler. I can handle it better that way. If I write everything down, it slows things up."

"Of course," he said.

"Suppose you *were* Notified, and suppose I'm the first one Taunton knocks off—what happens to Venus Project?"

"You may have a point," he admitted. "I'll level with you, Mitch. There has been no Notification."

"Thanks, Fowler," I said sincerely. "I *did* get shot at. And that accident in Washington—maybe it wasn't an accident. You don't imagine Taunton would try anything without Notifying you, do you?"

"I haven't provoked them to that extent, and they'd never do a thing like that anyhow. They're cheap, they're crooked, but they know the rules of the game. Killing in an industrial feud is a misdemeanor. Killing *without* Notification is a *commercial offense*. You haven't been getting into any of the wrong beds, shall I say?"

"No," I said. "My life's been very dull. The whole thing's crazy. It must have been a mistake. But I'm glad that whoever-it-was couldn't shoot."

"So am I, Mitch, so am I! Enough of your personal life. We've got business. You saw O'Shea?" He had already dismissed the shooting from his mind.

"I did. He's coming up here today. He'll be working closely with me."

"Splendid! Some of that glory will rub off on Fowler Schocken Associates if we play our cards right. Dig into it, Mitch. I don't have to tell you how."

It was a dismissal.

O'Shea was waiting in the anteroom of my office. It wasn't an ordeal; most of the female personnel was clustered around him as he sat perched on a desk, talking gruffly and authoritatively. There was no mistaking the looks in their eyes. He was a thirty-five-inch midget, but he had money and fame, the two things we drill and drill into the population. O'Shea could have taken his pick of them. I wondered how many he had picked since his return to Earth in a blaze of glory.

We run a taut office, but the girls didn't scatter until I cleared my throat.

"Morning, Mitch," O'Shea said. "You over your shock?"

"Sure. And I ran right into another one. Somebody tried to shoot me." I told the story and he grunted thoughtfully.

"Have you considered getting a bodyguard?" he asked.

"Of course. But I won't. It must have been a mistake."

"Like that cargo nacelle?"

I paused. "Jack, can we *please* get off this subject? It gives me the horrors."

"Permission granted," he beamed. "Now, let's go to work—and on what?"

"First, words. We want words that are about Venus, words that'll tickle people. Make them sit up. Make them muse about change, and space, and other worlds. Words to make them a little discontented with what they are and a little hopeful about what they might be. Words to make them feel noble about feeling the way they do and make them happy about the existence of Indiastries and Starrzelius Verily and Fowler Schocken Associates. Words that will do all these things and also make them feel unhappy about the existence of Universal Products and Taunton Associates."

He was staring at me with his mouth open. "You aren't serious," he finally exclaimed.

"You're on the inside now," I said simply. "That's the way we work. That's the way we worked on you."

46

"What are you talking about?"

"You're wearing Starrzelius Verily clothes and shoes, Jack. It means we got you. Taunton and Universal worked on you, Starrzelius and Schocken worked on you—and you chose Starrzelius. We reached you. Smoothly, without your ever being aware that it was happening, you became persuaded that there was something rather nice about Starrzelius clothes and shoes and that there was something rather not-nice about Universal clothes and shoes."

"I never read the ads," he said defiantly.

I grinned. "Our ultimate triumph is wrapped up in that statement," I said.

"I solemnly promise," O'Shea said, "that as soon as I get back to my hotel room I'll send my clothes down the incinerator chute—"

"Luggage too?" I asked. "Starrzelius luggage?"

He looked startled for a moment and then regained his calm. "Starrzelius luggage too," he said. "And then I'll pick up the phone and order a complete set of Universal luggage and apparel. And you can't stop me."

"I wouldn't dream of stopping you, Jack! It means more business for Starrzelius. Tell you what you're going to do: you'll get your complete set of Universal luggage and apparel. You'll use the luggage and wear the apparel for a while with a vague, submerged discontent. It's going to work on your libido, because our ads for Starrzelius—even though you say you don't read them—have convinced you that it isn't quite virile to trade with any other firm. Your self-esteem will suffer; deep down you'll *know* that you're not wearing the best. Your subconscious won't stand up under much of that. You'll find yourself 'losing' bits of Universal apparel. You'll find yourself 'accidentally' putting your foot through the cuff of your Universal pants. You'll find yourself over-packing the Universal luggage and damning it for not being roomier. You'll walk into stores and in a fit of momentary amnesia regarding this con-versation you'll buy Starrzelius, bless you."

O'Shea laughed uncertainly. "And you did it with words?"

"Words and pictures. Sight and sound and smell and taste and touch. And the greatest of these is words. Do you read poetry?"

"My God, of course not! Who can?"

"I don't mean the contemporary stuff; you're quite right about that. I mean Keats, Swinburne, Wylie—the great lyricists."

"I used to," he cautiously admitted. "What about it?"

"I'm going to ask you to spend the morning and afternoon with one of the world's great lyric poets: a girl named Tildy Mathis. She doesn't know that she's a poet; she thinks she's a boss copywriter. Don't enlighten her. It might make her unhappy.

'Thou still unravish'd bride of quietness,
    Thou foster-child of Silence and slow Time—'

That's the sort of thing she would have written before the rise of advertising. The correlation is perfectly clear. Advertising up, lyric poetry down. There are only so many people capable of put-ting together words that stir and move and sing. When it became possible to earn a very good liv-ing in advertising by exercising this capability, lyric poetry was left to untalented screwballs who

48

had to shriek for attention and compete by eccentricity."

"Why are you telling me all this?" he asked.

"I said you're on the inside, Jack. There's a responsibility that goes with the power. Here in this profession we reach into the souls of men and women. We do it by taking talent and—redirecting it. Nobody should play with lives the way we do unless he's motivated by the highest ideals."

"I get you," he said softly. "Don't worry about my motives. I'm not in this thing for money or fame. I'm in it so the human race can have some elbow room and dignity again." Jack's in it for ... humanity

"That's it," I said, putting on Expression Number One. But inwardly I was startled. The "highest ideal" I had been about to cite was Sales.

I buzzed for Tildy. "Talk to her," I said. "Answer her questions. Ask her some. Make it a long, friendly chat. Make her share your experiences. And, without knowing it, she'll write lyric fragments of your experiences that will go right to the hearts and souls of the readers. Don't hold out on her."

"Certainly not. Uh, Mitch, will she hold out on me?"

The expression on his face was from a Tanagra figurine of a hopeful young satyr.

"She won't," I promised solemnly. Everybody knew about Tildy. had a bad rep?

That afternoon, for the first time in four months, Kathy called me.

"Is anything wrong?" I asked sharply. "Anything I can do?"

She giggled. "Nothing wrong, Mitch. I just

49

wanted to say hello and tell you thanks for a lovely evening."

"How about another one?" I asked promptly.

"Dinner at my place tonight suit you?"

"It certainly does. It certainly, certainly does. What color dress will you be wearing? I'm going to buy you a real flower!"

"Oh, Mitch, you needn't be extravagant. We aren't courting and I already know you have more money than God. But there *is* something I wish you'd bring."

"Only name it."

"Jack O'Shea. Can you manage it? I saw by the 'cast that he came into town this morning and I suppose he's working with you."

Very dampened, I said: "Yes, he is. I'll check with him and call you back. You at the hospital?"

"Yes. And thanks so much for trying. I'd love to meet him."

I got in touch with O'Shea in Tildy's office. "You booked up for tonight?" I asked.

"Hmmm . . . I *could* be," he said. O'Shea was evidently learning about Tildy too.

"Here's my proposition. Quiet dinner at home with my wife and me. She happens to be beautiful and a good cook and a first-rate surgeon and excellent company."

"You're on."

So I called Kathy back and told her I'd bring the social lion about seven.

He stalked into my office at six, grumbling: "I'd better get a good meal out of this, Mitch. Your Miss Mathis appeals to me. What a dope! Does she have sense enough to come in out of the smog?"

"I don't believe so," I said. "But Keats was

50

properly hooked by a designing wench, and Byron didn't have sense enough to stay out of the venereal ward. Swinburne made a tragic mess out of his life. Do I have to go on?"

"Please, no. What kind of marriage have you got?"

"Interlocutory," I said, a little painfully in spite of myself.

He raised his eyebrows a trifle. "Maybe it's just the way I was brought up, but there's something about those arrangements that sets my teeth on edge."

"Mine too," I said, "at least in my own case. In case Tildy missed telling you, my beautiful and talented wife doesn't want to finalize it, we don't live together, and unless I change her mind in four months we'll be washed up."

"Tildy did miss telling me," he said. "You're pretty sick about it, seems to me."

I almost gave in to self-pity. I almost invited his sympathy. I almost started to tell him how rough it was, how much I loved her, how she wasn't giving me an even break, how I'd tried everything I could think of and nothing would convince her. And then I realized that I'd be telling it to a sixty-pound midget who, if he married, might become at any moment his wife's helpless plaything or butt of ridicule.

"Middling sick," I said. "Let's go, Jack. Time for a drink and then the shuttle."

Kathy had never looked lovelier, and I wished I hadn't let her talk me out of shooting a couple of days' pay on a corsage at Cartier's.

She said hello to O'Shea and he announced loudly and immediately: "I like you. There's no gleam in your eye. No 'Isn't he cute?' gleam. No. 'My, he must be rich and frustrated!' gleam. No 'A girl's got a right to try anything once' gleam. In short, you like me and I like you."

As you may have gathered, he was a little drunk.

"You are going to have some coffee, Mr. O'Shea," she said. "I ruined myself to provide real pork sausages and real apple sauce, and you're going to taste them."

"Coffee?" he said. "Coffiest for me, ma'am. To drink coffee would be disloyal to the great firm of Fowler Schocken Associates with which I am associated. Isn't that right, Mitch?"

"I give absolution this once," I said. "Besides, Kathy doesn't believe the harmless alkaloid in Coffiest is harmless." Luckily she was in the kitchen corner with her back turned when I said that, and either missed it or could afford to pretend she did. We'd had a terrific four-hour battle over that very point, complete with epithets like "baby-poisoner" and "crackpot reformer" and a few others that were shorter and nastier.

The coffee was served and quenched O'Shea's mild glow. Dinner was marvelous. Afterward, we all felt more relaxed.

"You've been to the Moon, I suppose?" Kathy asked O'Shea.

"Not yet. One of these days."

"There's nothing there," I said. "It's a waste of time. One of our dullest, deadest accounts. I suppose we only kept it for the experience we'd get, looking ahead to Venus. A few thousand people mining—that's the *whole* story."

"Excuse me," O'Shea said, and retired.

I grabbed the chance. "Kathy, darling," I said,

"It was very sweet of you to ask me over. Does it mean anything?"

She rubbed her right thumb and index finger together, and I knew that whatever she would say after that would be a lie. "It might, Mitch," she lied gently. "You'll have to give me time."

I threw away my secret weapon. "You're lying," I said disgustedly. "You always do this before you lie to me—I don't know about other people." I showed her, and she let out a short laugh.

"Fair's fair," she said with bitter amusement. "You always catch your breath and look right into my eyes when you lie to me—I don't know about your clients and fellow-employees."

O'Shea returned and felt the tension at once. "I ought to be going," he said. "Mitch, do we leave together?"

Kathy nodded, and I said: "Yes."

There were the usual politenesses at the door, and Kathy kissed me good night. It was a long, warm, clinging kiss; altogether the kind of kiss that should start the evening rather than end it. It set her own pulse going—I felt that!—but she coolly closed the door on us.

"You thought about a bodyguard again?" O'Shea asked.

"It was a mistake," I said stubbornly.

"Let's stop by your place for a drink," he said ingenuously.

The situation was almost pathetic. Sixty-pound Jack O'Shea was bodyguarding me. "Sure," I said. We got on the shuttle.

He went into the room first and turned on the light, and nothing happened. While sipping a very weak whisky and soda, he drifted around the place checking window locks, hinges, and the

53

like. "This chair would look better over there," he said. "Over there," of course, was out of the line of fire from the window. I moved it.

"Take care of yourself, Mitch," he said when he left. "That lovely wife and your friends would miss you if anything happened."

The only thing that happened was that I barked my shin setting up the bed, and that was happening all the time. Even Kathy, with a surgeon's neat, economical movements, bore the battle scars of life in a city apartment. You set up the bed at night, you took it down in the morning, you set up the table for breakfast, you took it down to get to the door. No wonder some short-sighted people sighed for the spacious old days, I thought, settling myself luxuriously for the night.

small living quarters

5

THINGS WERE
rolling within a week. With Runstead out of my hair and at work on the PregNot–A.I.G. hassle, I could really grip the reins.

Tildy's girls and boys were putting out the

copy—temperamental kids, sometimes doing a line a day with anguish; sometimes rolling out page after page effortlessly, with shining eyes, as though possessed. She directed and edited their stuff and passed the best of the best to me: nine-minute commercial scripts, pix cutlines, articles for planting, news stories, page ads, whispering campaign cuelines, endorsements, jokes-limericks-and-puns (clean and dirty) to float through the country.

Visual was hot. The airbrush and camera people were having fun sculpturing a planet. It was the ultimate in "Before and After" advertising, and they were caught by the sense of history.

Development kept pulling rabbits out of hats. Collier once explained to me when I hinted that he might be overoptimistic: "It's *energy,* Mr. Courtenay. Venus has got *energy.* It's closer to the sun. The sun pours all that energy into the planet in the form of heat and molecular bonds and fast particles. Here on Earth we don't have that level of tappable energy. We use windmills to tap the kinetic energy of the atmosphere. On Venus we'll use *turbines.* If we want electricity on Venus we'll just build an accumulator, put up a lightning rod and jump back. It's an entirely different *level.*"

Market Research-Industrial Anthropology was at work in San Diego sampling the Cal-Mex area, trying Tildy's copy, Visual's layouts and films and extrapolating and interpolating. I had a direct wire to the desk of Ham Harris, Runstead's vice, in San Diego.

A typical day began with a Venus Section meeting: pep talk by me, reports of progress by all hands, critique and cross-department suggestions.

Harris, on the wire, might advise Tildy that "serene atmosphere" wasn't going well as a cue phrase in his sampling and that she should submit a list of alternatives. Tildy might ask Collier whether it would be okay to say "topaz sands" in a planted article which would hint that Venus was crawling with uncut precious and semiprecious stones. Collier might tell Visual that they'd have to make the atmosphere redder in a "Before" panorama. And I might tell Collier to lay off because it was permissible license.

After adjournment everybody would go into production and I'd spend my day breaking ties, co-ordinating, and interpreting my directives from above down to the operational level. Before close of day we'd hold another meeting, which I would keep to some specific topic, such as: integration of Starrzelius products into the Venus economy, or income-level of prospective Venus colonists for optimum purchasing power twenty years after landing.

And then came the best part of the day. Kathy and I were going steady again. We were still under separate cover, but I was buoyantly certain that it wouldn't be long now. Sometimes she dated me, sometimes I dated her. We just went out and had fun eating well, drinking well, dressing well, and feeling that we were two good-looking people enjoying life. There wasn't much serious talk. She didn't encourage it and I didn't press it. I thought that time was on my side. Jack O'Shea made the rounds with us once before he had to leave for a lecture in Miami, and that made me feel good too. A couple of well-dressed, good-looking people who were so high-up they could

56

superficial goodness

entertain the world's number one celebrity. Life was good.

After a week of solid, satisfying progress on the job I told Kathy it was time for me to visit the outlying installations—the rocket site in Arizona and sampling headquarters in San Diego.

"Fine," she said. "Can I come along?"

I was silly-happy about it; it wouldn't be long now.

The rocket visit was routine. I had a couple of people there as liaison with Armed Forces, Republic Aviation, Bell Telephone Labs, and U. S. Steel. They showed Kathy and me through the monster, glib as tourist guides: ". . . vast steel shell . . . more cubage than the average New York office building . . . closed-cycle food and water and air regeneration . . . one-third drive, one-third freight, one-third living space . . . heroic pioneers . . . insulation . . . housekeeping power . . . sunside-darkside heat pumps . . . unprecedented industrial effort . . . national sacrifice . . . national security . . ."

Oddly, the most impressive thing about it to me was not the rocket itself but the wide swathe around it. For a full mile the land was cleared: no houses, no greenhouse decks, no food tanks, no sun traps. Partly security, partly radiation. The gleaming sand cut by irrigation pipes looked strange. There probably wasn't another sight like it in North America. It troubled my eyes. Not for years had I focused them more than a few yards.

"How strange," Kathy said at my side. "Could we walk out there?"

"Sorry, Dr. Nevin," said one of the liaison men.

57

"It's a deadline. The tower guards are ordered to shoot anybody out there."

"Have contrary orders issued," I said. "Dr. Nevin and I want to take a walk."

"Of course, Mr. Courtenay," the man said, very worried. "I'll do my best, but it'll take a little time. I'll have to clear it with C.I.C., Naval Intelligence, C.I.A., F.B.I., A.E.C. Security and Intelligence—"

I looked at Kathy, and she shrugged with helpless amusement. "Never mind," I said.

"Thank God!" breathed my liaison man. "Excuse me, Mr. Courtenay. It's never been done before so there aren't any channels to do it through. You know what *that* means."

"I do indeed," I said, from the heart. "Tell me, has all the security paid off?"

"It seems so, Mr. Courtenay. There's been no sabotage or espionage, foreign or Consie, that we know of." He rapped a knuckle of his right hand solemnly on a handsome oak engagement ring he wore on the third finger of his left hand. I made a mental note to have his expense account checked up on. A man on his salary had no business wearing that kind of jewelry.

"The Consies interested?" I asked.

"Who knows? C.I.C., C.I.A. and A.E.C. S&I. say yes. Naval Intelligence, F.B.I. and SS. say no. Would you like to meet Commander MacDonald? He's the O.N.I. chief here. A specialist in Consies."

"Like to meet a Consie specialist, Kathy?" I asked.

"If we have time," she said.

"I'll have them hold the jet for you if necessary," the liaison man said eagerly, trying hard to undo his fiasco on the tower guards. He led us through the tangle of construction shacks and warehouses to the administration building and past seven security check points to the office of the commander.

MacDonald was one of those career officers who make you feel good about being an American citizen—quiet, competent, strong. I could see from his insignia and shoulder flashes that he was a Contract Specialist, Intelligence, on his third five-year option from the Pinkerton Detective Agency. He was a regular; he wore the class ring of the Pinkerton Graduate School of Detection and Military Intelligence, Inc. It's pine with an open eye carved on it; no flashy inlay work. But it's like a brand name. It tells you that you're dealing with quality.

"You want to hear about Consies?" he asked quietly. "I'm your man. I've devoted my life to running them down."

"A personal grudge, Commander?" I asked, thinking I'd hear something melodramatic.

"No. Old-fashioned pride of workmanship if anything. I like the thrill of the chase, too, but there isn't much chasing. You get Consies by laying traps. Did you hear about the Topeka bombing? Of-course-I-shouldn't-knock-the-competition-but those guards should have known it was a setup for a Consie demonstration."

"Why, exactly, Commander?" Kathy asked.

He smiled wisely. "Feel," he said. "The kind of thing it's hard to put over in words. The Consies don't like hydraulic mining—ever. Give them a chance to parade their dislike and they'll take it if they can."

"But *why* don't they like hydraulic mining?"

she persisted. "We've got to have coal and iron, don't we?"

"Now," he said with pretended, humorous weariness, "you're asking me to probe the mind of a Consie. I've had them in the wrecking room for up to six hours at a stretch and never yet have they talked sense. If I caught the Topeka Consie, say, he'd talk willingly—but it would be gibberish. He'd tell me the hydraulic miner was destroying topsoil. I'd say yes, and what about it. He'd say, well can't you *see?* I'd say, see what? He'd say, the topsoil can never be replaced. I'd say, yes it can if it had to be and anyway tank farming's better. He'd say something like tank farming doesn't provide animal cover and so on. It always winds up with him telling me the world's going to hell in a hand-basket and people have got to be made to realize it—and me telling him we've always got along somehow and we'll keep going somehow."

Kathy laughed incredulously and the commander went on: "They're fools, but they're *tough*. They have discipline. A cell system. If you get one Consie you always get the two or three others in his cell, but you hardly ever get any more. There's no lateral contact between cells, and vertical contact with higher-ups is by rendezvous with middlemen. Yes, I think I know them and that's why I'm not especially worried about sabotage or a demonstration here. It doesn't have the right ring to it."

Kathy and I lolled back watching the commercials parade around the passenger compartment of the jet at eye level. There was the good old Kiddiebutt jingle I worked out many years ago when

I was a trainee. I nudged Kathy and told her about it as it blinked and chimed Victor Herbert's *Toyland* theme at us.

All the commercials went blank and a utility announcement, without sound effects, came on.

> *In Compliance With Federal Law, Passengers Are Advised That They Are Now Passing Over The San Andreas Fault Into Earthquake Territory, And That Earthquake Loss And Damage Clauses In Any Insurance They May Carry Are Now Canceled And Will Remain Canceled Until Passengers Leave Earthquake Territory.*

Then the commercials resumed their parade.

"And," said Kathy, "I suppose it says in the small print that yak-bite insurance is good anywhere except in Tibet."

"Yak-bite insurance?" I asked, astonished. "What on earth do you carry that for?"

"A girl can never tell when she'll meet an unfriendly yak, can she?"

"I conclude that you're kidding," I said with dignity. "We ought to land in a few minutes. Personally, I'd like to pop in on Ham Harris unexpectedly. He's a good kid, but Runstead may have infected him with defeatism. There's nothing worse in our line."

"I'll come along with you if I may, Mitch."

We gawked through the windows like tourists as the jet slid into the traffic pattern over San Diego and circled monotonously waiting for its calldown from the tower. Kathy had never been there before. I had been there once, but there's always something new to see because buildings are always falling down and new ones being put up. And what buildings! They're more like plastic tents on plastic skeletons than anything else. That kind of construction means they give and sway when a quake jiggles southern California instead of snapping and crumbling. And if the quake is bad enough and the skeleton does snap, what have you lost? Just some plastic sheeting that broke along the standard snap grooves and some plastic structural members that may or may not be salvageable.

From a continental economic viewpoint, it's also a fine idea not to tie up too much fancy construction in southern California. Since the H-bomb tests did things to the San Andreas fault, there's been a pretty fair chance that the whole area would slide quietly into the Pacific some day—any day. But when we looked down out of the traffic pattern, it still was there and, like everybody else, we knew that it would probably stay there for the duration of our visit. Before my time there had been some panic when the quakes became daily, but I'd blame that on the old-style construction that fell hard and in jagged hunks. Eventually people got used to it and—as you'd expect in southern California—even proud of it. Natives could cite you reams of statistics to prove that you stand more chance of being struck by lightning or a meteorite than you do of getting killed in one of their quakes.

We got a speedy three-man limousine to whisk us to the local branch of Fowler Schocken Associates. My faint uneasiness about Market Research extended to the possibility that Ham Harris might have a tipster at the airport to give him time to tidy up for a full-dress inspection. And that kind of thing is worse than useless.

The receptionist gave me my first setback. She didn't recognize my face and she didn't recognize my name when I gave it to her. She said lazily: "I'll see if Mr. Harris is busy, Mr. Connelly."

"Mr. Courtenay, young lady. And I'm Mr. Harris's boss." Kathy and I walked in on a scene of idleness and slackness that curled my hair.

Harris, with his coat off, was playing cards with two young employees. Two more were gaping, glassy-eyed, before a hypnoteleset, obviously in trance state. Another man was lackadaisically punching a calculator, one-finger system.

"Harris!" I thundered.

Everybody except the two men in trance swiveled my way, open-mouthed. I walked to the hypnoteleset and snapped it off. They came to, groggily.

"Mum-mum-mum-mister Courtenay," Harris stuttered. "We didn't expect—"

"Obviously. The rest of you, carry on. Harris, let's go into your office." Unobtrusively, Kathy followed us.

"Harris," I said, "good work excuses a lot. We've been getting damn good work out of you on this project. I'm disturbed, gravely disturbed, by the atmosphere here. But that can be corrected—"

His phone rang, and I picked it up.

A voice said excitedly: "Ham? He's here. Make it snappy; he took a limousine."

"Thanks," I said and hung up. "Your tipster at the airport," I told Harris. He went white. "Show me your tally sheets," I said. "Your interview forms. Your punchcard codes. Your masters. Your sigma-progress charts. The works. Everything, in

63

short, that you wouldn't expect me to ask to see. *Get them out.*"

He stood there a long, long time and finally said: "There aren't any."

"What have you got to show me?"

"Finalizations," he muttered. "Composites."

"Fakes, you mean? Fiction, like the stuff you've been feeding us over the wire?"

He nodded. His face was sick.

"How could you do it, Harris?" I demanded. *"How—could—you—do it?"*

He poured out a confused torrent of words. He hadn't meant to. It was his first independent job. Maybe he was just no damn good. He'd tried to keep the lower personnel up to snuff while he was dogging it himself but it couldn't be done; they sensed it and took liberties and you didn't dare check them up. His self-pitying note changed; he became weakly belligerent. What difference did it make anyway? It was just preliminary paperwork. One man's guess was as good as another's. And anyway the whole project might go down the drain. What if he had been taking it easy; he bet there were plenty of other people who took it easy and everything came out all right anyway.

"No," I said. "You're wrong and you ought to know you're wrong. Advertising's an art, but it depends on the sciences of sampling, area-testing, and customer research. You've knocked the props from under our program. We'll salvage what we can and start again."

He took a feeble stand: "You're wasting your time if you do that, Mr. Courtenay. I've been working closely with Mr. Runstead for a long time. I know what he thinks, and he's as big a shot as you are. He thinks this paperwork is just a lot of expensive nonsense."

I knew Matt Runstead better than that. I knew he was sound and so did everybody else. "What," I asked sharply, "have you got to back that statement up with? Letters? Memos? Taped calls?"

"I must have something like that," he said, and dived into his desk. He flipped through letters and memos, and played snatches of tape for minutes while the look of fear and frustration on his face deepened. At last he said in bewilderment: "I can't seem to find anything—but I'm *sure*—"

Sure he was sure. The highest form of our art is to convince the customer without letting him know he's being convinced. This weak sister had been indoctrinated by Runstead with the unrealistic approach and then sent in on my project, to do a good job of bitching it up.

"You're fired, Harris," I said. "Get out and don't come back. And I wouldn't advise you to try for a job in the advertising profession after this."

I went out into the office and announced: "You're through. All of you. Collect your personal stuff and leave the office. You'll get your checks by mail."

They gaped. Beside me, Kathy murmured: "Mitch, is that really necessary?"

"You're damned right it's necessary. Did one of them tip off the home office on what was going on? No; they just relaxed and drifted. I said it was an infection, didn't I? This is it." Ham Harris drifted past us toward the door, hurt bewilderment on his face. He had been *so* sure

Runstead would back him up. He had his crammed briefcase in one hand and his raincoat in the other. He didn't look at me.

I went into his vacated office and picked up the direct wire to New York. "Hester? This is Mr. Courtenay. I've just fired the entire San Diego branch. Notify Personnel and have them do whatever's necessary about their pay. And get me Mr. Runstead on the line."

I drummed my fingers impatiently for a long minute, and then Hester said: "Mr. Courtenay, I'm sorry to keep you waiting. Mr. Runstead's secretary says he's left for Little America on one of those tours. She says he cleaned up the A.I.G. thing and felt like a rest."

"Felt like a rest. Good God almighty. Hester, get me a New York to Little America reservation. I'm shooting right back on the next jet. I want to just barely touch ground before I zip off to the Pole. Got it?"

"Yes, Mr. Courtenay."

I hung up and found that Kathy was staring at me. "You know, Mitch," she said, "I've been uncharitable to you in my time. Kicking about your bad temper. I can see where you got it if this has been a typical operation."

"It's not typical," I said. "It's the worst case of flagrant obstructionism I've ever seen. But there's a lot of it. Everybody trying to make everybody else look bad. Darling, I've got to get to the field now and bull my way onto the next Eastbound. Do you want to come too?"

She hesitated. "You won't mind if I stay and do a little tourist stuff by myself?"

"No, of course not. You have a good time and when you get back to New York I'll be there."

We kissed, and I raced out. The office was clear by then and I told the building manager to lock it until further notice when Kathy left.

I looked up from the street and she waved at me from the strange, flimsy building.

Kathy real: zed he was behaving badly but still stuck w/ him

6

I SWUNG OFF the ramp at New York, and Hester was right there. "Good girl," I told her. "When's the Pole rocket shoot off?"

"Twelve minutes, from Strip Six, Mr. Courtenay. Here are your ticket and the reservation. And some lunch in case—"

"Fine. I did miss a meal." We headed for Strip Six, with me chewing a regenerated cheese sandwich as I walked. "What's up at the office?" I asked indistinctly.

"Big excitement about you firing the San Diego people. Personnel sent up a complaint to Mr. Schocken and he upheld you—approximately Force Four."

That wasn't too good. Force Twelve—hurricane —would have been a blast from his office on the order of: "How dare you housekeepers question the decision of a Board man working on his own project? Never let me catch you—" and so on. Force Four—rising gale, small craft make for harbor—was something like: "Gentlemen, I'm sure Mr. Courtenay had perfectly good reasons for doing what he did. Often the Big Picture is lost to the purely routine workers in our organization—"

I asked Hester: "Is Runstead's secretary just a hired hand or one of his—" I was going to say "stooges" but smoothly reversed my field "—one of his confidants?"

"She's pretty close to him," Hester said cautiously.

"What was her reaction to the San Diego business?"

"Somebody told me she laughed her head off, Mr. Courtenay."

I didn't push it any harder. Finding out where I stood with respect to the big guns was legitimate. Asking about the help was asking her to rat on them. Not that there weren't girls who did. "I expect to be right back," I told her. "All I want to do is straighten something out with Runstead."

"Your wife won't be along?" she asked.

"No. She's a doctor. I'm going to tear Runstead into five or six pieces; if Dr. Nevin were along she might try to put them back together again."

Hester laughed politely and said: "Have a pleasant trip, Mr. Courtenay." We were at the ramp on Strip Six.

It wasn't a pleasant trip; it was a miserable trip on a miserable, undersized tourist rocket. We flew low, and there were prism windows at all seats, which never fail to make me airsick. You turn your head and look out and you're looking straight *down*. Worse, all the ads were Taunton Associates jobs. You look out the window and just as you convince your stomach that everything's all right and yourself that it's interesting country below, wham: a sleazy, over-sexed Taunton ad for some crummy product opaques the window and one of their nagging, stupid jingles drills into your ear.

Over the Amazon valley we were running into some very interesting stuff, and I was inspecting Electric Three, which happens to be the world's biggest power dam, when, wham:

> *BolsterBra, BolsterBra,*
> *Bolsters all the way;*
> *Don't you crumple, don't you slumple;*
> *Keep them up to stay!*

The accompanying before-and-after live pix were in the worst possible taste, and I found myself thanking God again that I worked for Fowler Schocken Associates.

It was the same off Tierra del Fuego. We went off the great circle course for a look at the whale fisheries, vast sea areas enclosed by booms that let the plankton in and didn't let the whales out. I was watching with fascination as a cow whale gave suck to her calf—it looked something like an aerial refueling operation—when the window opaqued again for another dose of Taunton shock treatment:

> *Sister, do you smell like this to your mister?*

The olfactory went on, and it was the very last straw. I had to use my carton while the ad chirped:

> *No wonder he's hard to get! Use Swett!*

and one of those heavenly-harmony trios caroled in waltz time:

> *Perspire, perspire, perspire,*
> *But don't—kill off his desire—*

and then a gruff, prose, medical pitch:

DON'T TRY TO STOP PERSPIRATION.

IT'S SUICIDE. DOCTORS ADVISE

A DEODORANT AND NOT AN ASTRINGENT

and then back to the first line and the olfactory. This time it made no difference; I had nothing more to give.

Taunton's was great on the gruff medical pitch; you'd think they invented it.

My seatmate, a nondescript customer in Universal apparel, watched with a little amusement as I retched. "Too much for you, friend?" he asked, showing the maddening superiority people who suffer from motion-sickness know too well.

"Uh," I said.

"Some of those ads are enough to make anybody sick," he said, greatly encouraged by my brilliant riposte.

Well, I couldn't let that get by. "Exactly what do you mean by that remark?" I asked evenly.

It frightened him. "I only meant that it smelled a little strong," he said hastily. "Just that particular ad. I didn't mean ads in general. There's nothing wrong with *me,* my friend!"

"Good for you," I said, and turned away.

He was still worried, and told me: "I'm perfectly sound, friend. I come from a good family, I went to a good school. I'm in the production end myself—die-maker in Philly—but I know the stuff's got to be sold. Channels of distribution. Building markets. Vertical integration. See? I'm perfectly sound!"

"Okay," I grunted. "Then watch your mouth."

He shriveled into his half of the seat. I hadn't enjoyed squelching him, but it was a matter of principle. He should have known better.

We were held up over Little America while a couple of other tourist craft touched down. One of them was Indian and I mellowed at the sight. That ship, from nose to tail, was Indiastry-built. The crewmen were Indiastry-trained and Indiastry-employed. The passengers, waking and sleeping, paid tribute minute by minute to Indiastry. And Indiastry paid tribute to Fowler Schocken Associates.

A tow truck hauled us into the great double-walled plastic doughnut that is Little America. There was only one check point. Little America is an invisible export—a dollar trap for the tourists of the world, with no military aspects. (There are Polar military bases, but they are small, scattered, and far under the ice.) A small thorium reactor heats and powers the place. Even if some nation desperate for fissionable material were to try and get it, they wouldn't have anything of military value. Windmills eke out the thorium reactor, and there's some "heat pump" arrangement that I don't understand which ekes out the windmills.

At the check point I asked about Runstead. The officer looked him up and said: "He's on the two-day tour out of New York. Thomas Cook and Son. His quarters are III–C–2205." He pulled out a map of the place and showed me that this meant third ring in, third floor up, fifth sector, twenty-second room. "You can't miss it. I can accommodate you with a nearby room, Mr. Courtenay—"

"Thanks. Later." I shoved off and elbowed my

way through crowds chattering in a dozen languages to III–C–2205 and rang the bell. No answer.

A pleasant young man said to me: "I'm Mr. Cameron, the tour director. Can I help you?"

"Where's Mr. Runstead? I want to see him on business."

"Dear me. We try to get away from all that— I'll look in my register if you'll just wait a moment."

He took me to his office-bedroom-bath up the sector a way and pawed through a register. "The Starrzelius Glacier climb," he said. "Dear me. He went alone. Left at 0700, checked out in electric suit with R.D.F. and rations. He should be back in five hours or so. Have you arranged for quarters yet, Mr.—?"

"Not yet. I want to go after Runstead. It's urgent." And it was. I was going to burst a blood vessel if I didn't get my hands on him.

The slightly fluttery tour director spent about five minutes convincing me that the best thing for me to do was sign on for his tour and he'd arrange *everything*. Otherwise I'd be shifted from pillar to post buying and renting necessary equipment from concessionaires and then as like as not be turned back at checkout and not be able to find the concessionaires again while my vacation was ticking away. I signed on and he beamed. He gave me a room in the sector—plenty of luxury. It would have been twelve by eighteen if it hadn't been slightly wedge-shaped.

In five minutes he was dealing out equipment to me. "Power pack—strap it on *so*. That's the only thing that can go wrong; if you have a power failure take a sleepy pill and don't worry. You'll

72

freeze, but we'll pick you up before there's tissue damage. Boots. Plug them in *so*. Gloves. Plug them in. Coveralls. Hood. Snowglasses. Radio direction finder. Just tell the checkout guard 'Starrzelius Glacier' and he'll set it. Two simple switches plainly labeled 'Out' and 'In.' Outward bound it goes 'beep-*beep*'—ascending. Inward bound it goes '*beep*-beep'—descending. Just remember, going *up* the glacier, the tone goes *up*. Going *down* the glacier, the tone goes *down*. Distress signal—a big red handle. You just pull and immediately you start broadcasting. The planes will be out in fifteen minutes. You have to pay expenses for the search and rescue, so I *wouldn't* yank the handle just for a ride back. It's always possible to rest, have a sip of Coffiest, and keep on going. Route-marked map. Snowshoes. Gyrocompass. And rations. Mr. Courtenay, you are equipped. I'll lead you to checkout."

The outfit wasn't as bad as it sounded. I've been more heavily bundled up against the lakeside winds in a Chicago winter. The lumpy items, like the power pack, the R.D.F., and the rations, were well distributed. The snowshoes folded into a pair of staffs with steel points for ice climbing, and went into a quiver on my back.

Checkout was very thorough. They started with my heart and worked through my equipment, with particular emphasis on the power pack. I passed, and they set the R.D.F. for Starrzelius Glacier, with many more warnings not to overdo it.

It wasn't cold, not inside the suit. For a moment only I opened the face flap. *Wham!* I closed it again. Forty below, they had told me—a foolish-sounding figure until my nose felt it for a split second. I didn't need the snow shoes at the base of the towering plastic doughnut; it was crust ice that my spike-soled shoes bit into. I oriented the map with the little gyrocompass and trudged off into the vast whiteness along the proper bearing. From time to time I pressed my left sleeve, squeezing the molded R.D.F. switch, and heard inside my hood a cheerful, reassuring "Beep-*beep*. Beep-*beep*. Beep-*beep*."

There were some score people frolicking in one party I passed and waved cheerily at. They seemed to be Chinese or Indians. What an adventure it must be for them! But, like indifferent swimmers hugging a raft, they did their frolicking almost under the shadow of Little America. Farther out there were some people playing a game I didn't know. They had posts with bottomless baskets set up at either end of a marked-off rectangular field, and the object was to toss a large silicone ball through the baskets. Still farther out there was a large skiing class with instructors in red suits.

I looked back after trudging for what seemed only a few minutes and couldn't see the red suits any more. I couldn't see details of Little America —just a gray-white shadow. "Beep-*beep*," my R. D.F. said and I kept going. Runstead was going to hear from me. Soon.

The aloneness was eerie but not—not unpleasant. Little America was no longer visible behind me, not even as a gray-white blur. And I didn't care. Was this how Jack O'Shea felt? Was this why he fumbled for words to describe Venus and was never satisfied with the words he found?

My feet plunged into a drift, and I unshipped and opened the snowshoes. They snapped on, and after a little stumbling experiment, I fell into an easy, sliding shuffle that was a remarkably pleasant way of covering ground. It wasn't floating. But neither was it the solid jar of a shoe sole against a paved surface—all the walking I had known for thirty-odd years.

I marched the compass course by picking landmarks and going to them: an oddly-recurved ice hummock, a blue shadow on a swale of snow. The R.D.F. continued to confirm me. I was blown up with pride at my mastery of the wild, and after two hours I was wildly hungry all at once.

What I had to do was squat and open a silicone-tissue bell into which I fitted. Exposing my nose cautiously from time to time I judged the air warm enough in five minutes. I ravenously gulped self-heated stew and tea and tried to smoke a cigarette. On the second puff the little tent was thoroughly smoked and I was blinded with tears. Regretfully I put it out against my shoe, closed my face mask, stowed the tent, and stretched happily.

After another bearing I started off again. Hell, I told myself. This Runstead thing is just a difference of temperament. He can't see the wide-open spaces and you can. There's no malice involved. He just thinks it's a crackpot idea because he doesn't realize that there are people who go for it. All you've got to do is *explain* it—

That argument, born of well-being, crumbled at one touch of reason. Runstead was out on the glacier too. He most certainly could see the wide-open spaces if, of all the places on earth he could be, he chose the Starrzelius Glacier. Well, a show-down would shortly be forthcoming. "Beep-*beep*."

I sighted through the compass and picked a

black object that was dead on my course. I couldn't quite make it out, but it was visible and it wasn't moving. I broke into a shuffling run that made me pant, and against my will I slowed down. It was a man.

When I was twenty yards away, the man looked impatiently at his watch, and I broke into the clumsy run again.

"Matt!" I said. "Matt Runstead!"

"That's right, Mitch," he said, as nasty as ever. "You're sharp today." I looked at him very slowly and very carefully, phrasing my opening remarks. He had folded skiis thrust into the snow beside him.

"What's—what's—" I stammered.

"I have time to spare," he said, "but you've wasted enough of it. Good-by, Mitch." While I stood there dumbly he picked up his folded skiis, swung them into the air, and poleaxed me. I fell backwards with pain, bewilderment, and shamed rage bursting my head. I felt him fumbling at my chest and then I didn't feel anything for a while.

I woke thinking I had kicked the covers off and that it was cold for early autumn. Then the ice-blue Antarctic sky knifed into my eyes, and I felt the crumbly snow beneath me. It had happened, then. My head ached horribly and I was cold. Too cold. I felt and found that the power pack was missing. No heat to the suit, gloves, and boots. No power to the R.D.F. coming or going. No use to pull the emergency signal.

I tottered to my feet and felt the cold grip me like a vise. There were footprints punched into the snow leading away—where? There was the trail of my snowshoes. Stiffly I took a step back along that trail, and then another, and then another.

The rations. I could thrust them into the suit, break the heat seals, and let them fill the suit with temporary warmth. Plodding step by step I debated: stop and rest while you drink the ration's heat or keep moving? You need a rest, I told myself. Something impossible happened, your head is aching. You'll feel better if you sit for a moment, open a ration or two, and then go on.

I didn't sit. I knew what that would mean. Painful step after painful step I fumbled a Coffiest can from its pocket with fingers that would barely obey me, and fumbled it into my suit. My thumb didn't seem strong enough to pop the seal and I told myself: sit down for a moment and gather your strength. You don't have to lie down, pleasant as that would be . . . my thumb drove through the seal and the tingling heat was painful.

It became a blur. I opened more cans, and then I couldn't work them out of their pockets any more. I sat down at least once and got up again. And then I sat down, feeling guilty and ashamed of the indulgence, telling myself I'd get up in one more second for Kathy, two more seconds for Kathy, three more seconds for Kathy.

But I didn't.

7

I FELL ASLEEP
on a mountain of ice; I woke up in a throbbing,
strumming inferno, complete with red fire and
brutish-looking attendant devils. It was exactly
what I would have consigned a Taunton copysmith to. I was confused to find myself there.

The confusion did not last long. One of the
attendant devils shook my shoulder roughly and
said: "Gimme a hand, sleepy. I gotta stow my
hammock." My head cleared and it was very plain
that he was simply a lower-class consumer—perhaps a hospital attendant?

"Where's this?" I asked him. "Are we back in
Little America?"

"Jeez, you talk funny," he commented. "Gimme
a hand, will ya?"

"Certainly not!" I told him. "I'm a star-class
copysmith."

He looked at me pityingly, said "Punchy," and
went away into the strumming, red-lit darkness.

I stood up, swaying on my feet, and grabbed
an elbow hurrying past from darkness to dark-

ness. "Excuse me," I said. "Where is this place? Is it a hospital?"

The man was another consumer, worse-tempered than the first. "Leggo my yarm!" he snarled. I did. "Ya want on sick call, ya wait until we land," he said.

"Land?"

"Yah, land. Listen, Punchy, don't ya know what ya signed up for?"

"Signed up? No; I don't. But you're being too familiar. I'm a star-class copysmith—"

His face changed. "Ahah," he said wisely. "I can fix ya up. Justa minnit, Punchy. I'll be right back wit' the stuff."

He was, too. "The stuff" was a little green capsule. "Only five hunnerd," he wheedled. "Maybe the last one on board. Ya wanta touch down wit' the shakes? Nah! This'll straighten ya out fer landing—"

"Landing *where?*" I yelled. "What's all this about? I don't know, and I don't want your dope. Just tell me where I am and what I'm supposed to have signed up for and I'll take it from there!"

He looked at me closely and said: "Ya got it bad. A hit in the head, maybe? Well, Punchy, yer in the Number Six Hold of the Labor Freighter *Thomas R. Malthus.* Wind and weather, immaterial. Course, 273 degrees. Speed 300, destination Costa Rica, cargo slobs like you and me for the Chlorella plantations." It was the rigmarole of a relieved watch officer, or a savage parody of it.

"You're—" I hesitated.

"Downgraded," he finished bitterly, and stared at the green capsule in the palm of his hand. Abruptly he gulped it and went on: "I'm gonna hit the comeback trail, though." A sparkle crept into his eye. "I'm gonna introduce new and efficient methods in the plantations. I'll be a foreman in a week. I'll be works manager in a month. I'll be a director in a year. And then I'm gonna buy the Cunard Line and plate all their rockets with solid gold. Nothing but first-class accommodations. Nothing but the best for my passengers. I always kept her smooth on the Atlantic run. I'll build you a gold-plated imperial suite aboard my flag ship, Punchy. The best is none too good for my friend Punchy. If you don't like gold I'll get platinum. If you don't like—"

I inched away and he didn't notice. He kept babbling his hophead litany. It made me glad I'd never taken to the stuff. I came to a bulkhead and sat down hopelessly, leaning against it. Somebody sat down beside me and said "Hello there" in a cozy voice.

"Hello," I said. "Say, are we really headed for Costa? How can I get to see a ship's officer? This is all a mistake."

"Oh," said the man, "why worry about it? Live and let live. Eat, drink, and be merry is my motto."

"Take your God-damned hands off me!" I told him.

He became shrill and abusive, and I got up and walked on, stumbling over legs and torsos.

It occurred to me that I'd never really known any consumers except during the brief periods when they were serving me. It occurred to me that I'd casually accepted their homosexual component and exploited it without ever realizing what it reduced to in reality. I wanted very badly to get out of Number Six Hold. I wanted to get back to New York, find out what kind of stunt

Runstead had pulled and why, get back to Kathy, and my friendship with Jack O'Shea, and my big job at Fowler Schocken. I had things to do.

One of the red lights said Crash Emergency Exit. I thought of the hundreds of people jammed in the hold trying to crowd out through the door, and shuddered.

"Excuse me, my friend," somebody said hoarsely to me. "You'd better move." He began to throw up, and apparently containers weren't issued aboard labor freighters. I rolled the emergency door open and slid through.

"Well?" growled a huge Detective Agency guard.

"I want to see a ship's officer," I said. "I'm here by some mistake. My name is Mitchell Courtenay. I'm a copysmith with the Fowler Schocken Associates."

"The number," he snapped.

"16–156–187," I told him, and I admit that there was a little pride in my voice. You can lose money and health and friendship, but they can't take a low Social Security number away from you . . .

He was rolling up my sleeve, not roughly. The next moment I went spinning against the bulkhead with my face burning from a ham-handed slap. "Get back between decks, Punchy!" the guard roared. "Yer not on an excursion and I don't like yer funny talk!"

I stared incredulously at the pit of my elbow. The tattoo read: "1304–9974–1416–156–187723." My own number was buried in it, but the inks matched perfectly. The style of lettering was very slightly off—not enough for anybody to notice but me.

"Waddaya waitin' for?" the guard said. "You seen yer number before, ain't ya?"

"No," I said evenly, but my legs were quivering. I was scared—terribly scared. "I never saw this number before. It's been tattooed around my real number. I'm Courtenay, I tell you. I can prove it. I'll pay you—" I fumbled in my pockets and found no money. I abruptly realized that I was wearing a strange and shabby suit of Universal apparel, stained with food and worse.

"So pay," the guard said impassively.

"I'll pay you later," I told him. "Just get me to somebody responsible—"

A natty young flight lieutenant in Panagra uniform popped into the narrow corridor. "What's going on here?" he demanded of the guard. "The hatchway light's still on. Can't you keep order between decks? Your agency gets a fitness report from us, you know." He ignored me completely.

"I'm sorry, Mr. Kobler," the guard said, saluting and coming to a brace. "This man seems to be on the stuff. He came out and gave me an argument that he's a star-class copysmith on board by mistake—"

"Look at my number!" I yelled at the lieutenant.

His face wrinkled as I thrust my bared elbow under his nose. The guard grabbed me and snarled: "Don't you bother the—"

"Just a minute," said the Panagra officer. "I'll handle this. That's a high number, fellow. What do you expect to prove by showing me that?"

"It's been added to, fore and aft. My real number is 16–156–187. See? Before and after that there's a different lettering style! It's tampering!"

Holding his breath, the lieutenant looked very

closely. He said: "Umm. Just barely possible . . . come with me." The guard hastened to open a corridor door for him and me. He looked scared.

The lieutenant took me through a roaring confusion of engine rooms to the purser's hatbox-sized office. The purser was a sharp-faced gnome who wore his Panagra uniform as though it were a sack. "Show him your number," the lieutenant directed me, and I did. To the purser he said: "What's the story on this man?"

The purser slipped a reel into the reader and cranked it. "1304–9974–1416–156–187723," he read at last. "Groby, William George; 26; bachelor; broken home (father's desertion) child; third of five sibs; H-H balance, male 1; health, 2.9; occupational class 2 for seven years; 1.5 for three months; education 9; signed labor contract B." He looked up at the flight officer. "A very dull profile, lieutenant. Is there any special reason why I should be interested in this man?"

The lieutenant said: "He claims he's a copysmith in here by mistake. He says somebody altered his number. And he speaks a little above his class."

"Tut," said the purser. "Don't let that worry you. A broken-home child, especially a middle sib from the lower levels, reads and views incessantly trying to better himself. But you'll notice—"

"That's enough of that," I snarled at the little man, quite fed up. "I'm Mitchell Courtenay. I can buy you and sell you without straining my petty cash account. I'm in charge of the Fowler Schocken Associates Venus Section. I want you to get New York on the line immediately and we'll wind up this farce. Now jump, damn you!"

The flight lieutenant looked alarmed and reached for the phone, but the purser smiled and moved it away from his hand. "Mitchell Courtenay, are you?" he asked kindly. He reached for another reel and put it in the viewer. "Here we are," he said, after a little cranking. The lieutenant and I looked.

It was the front page of the *New York Times*. The first column contained the obituary of Mitchell Courtenay, head of Fowler Schocken Associates Venus Section. I had been found frozen to death on Starrzelius Glacier near Little America. I had been tampering with my power pack, and it had failed. I read on long after the lieutenant had lost interest. Matt Runstead was taking over Venus Section. I was a loss to my profession. My wife, Dr. Nevin, had refused to be interviewed. Fowler Schocken was quoted in a ripe eulogy of me. I was a personal friend of Venus Pioneer Jack O'Shea, who had expressed shock and grief at the news.

The purser said: "I picked that up in Capetown. Lieutenant, get this silly son of a bitch back between decks, will you please?"

The guard had arrived. He slapped and kicked me all the way back to Number Six Hold.

I caromed off somebody as the guard shoved me through the door into the red darkness. After the relatively clear air of the outside, the stink was horrible.

"What did you do?" the human cushion asked amiably, picking himself up.

"I tried to tell them who I am . . ." That wasn't going to get me anywhere. "What happens next?" I asked.

"We land. We get quarters. We get to work. What contract are you on?"

"Labor contract B, they said."

He whistled. "I guess they really had you, huh?"

"What do you mean? What's it all about?"

"Oh—you were blind, were you? Too bad. B contract's five years. For refugees, morons, and anybody else they can swindle into signing up. There's a conduct clause. I got offered the B, but I told them if that was the best they could do I'd just go out and give myself up to the Brink's Express. I talked them into an F contract—they must have needed help real bad. It's one year and I can buy outside the company stores and things like that."

I held my head to keep it from exploding. "It can't be such a bad place to work," I said. "Country life—farming—fresh air and sunshine."

"Um," said the man in an embarrassed way. "It's better than chemicals, I guess. Maybe not so good as mining. You'll find out soon enough."

He moved away, and I fell into a light doze when I should have been making plans.

There wasn't any landing-ready signal. We just hit, and hit hard. A discharge port opened, letting in blinding tropical sunlight. It was agony after the murky hold. What swept in with it was not country air but a gush of disinfectant aerosol. I untangled myself from a knot of cursing laborers and flowed with the stream toward the port.

"Hold it, stupid!" said a hard-faced man wearing a plant-protection badge. He threw a number plaque on a cord around my neck. Everybody got one and lined up at a table outside the ship. It was in the shadow of the Chlorella plantation, a towering eighty-story structure like office "In-and-Out" baskets stacked up to the sky. There were mirrored louvers at each tier. Surrounding the big building were acres of eye-stabbing glare. I realized that this was more mirrored louvers to catch the sun, bounce it off more mirrors inside the tiers and onto the photosynthesis tanks. It was a spectacular, though not uncommon, sight from the air. On the ground it was plain hell. I should have been planning, planning. But the channels of my mind were choked by: "From the sun-drenched plantations of Costa Rica, tended by the deft hands of independent farmers with pride in their work, comes the juicyripe goodness of Chlorella Proteins . . ." Yes; I had written those words.

"Keep moving!" a plant-protection man bawled. "Keep it moving, you God-damned scum-skimmers! Keep it moving!" I shaded my eyes and shuffled ahead as the line moved past the table. A dark-glassed man at the table was asking me: "Name?"

"Mitchell Court—"

"That's the one I told you about," said the purser's voice.

"Okay; thanks." To me: "Groby, we've had men try to bug out of a B Contract before this, you know. They're always sorry they tried. Do you know what the annual budget of Costa Rica is, by any chance?"

"No," I mumbled.

"It's about a hundred and eighty-three billion dollars. And do you happen to know what the annual taxes of Chlorella Corporation are?"

"No. Damn it, man—"

He broke in: "About a hundred and eighty billion dollars. From that, a bright fellow like you will conclude that the government—*and courts*—of Costa Rica do just about what Chlorella wants done. If we want to make an example of a contract-breaker they'll do it for us. Bet your life. Now, what's your name, Groby?"

"Groby," I said hoarsely.

"First name? Educational level? H-H balance?"

"I don't remember. But if you'll give them to me on a piece of paper I'll memorize them."

I heard the purser laugh and say: "He'll do."

"All right, Groby," the man in dark glasses said genially. "No harm done. Here's your profile and assignment. We'll make a skimmer out of you yet. Move on."

I moved on. A plant protection man grabbed my assignment and bawled at me: "Skimmers that way."

"That way" was under the bottom tier of the building, into light even more blinding, down a corridor between evil-smelling, shallow tanks, and at last through a door into the central pylon of the structure. There was a well-lit room which seemed twilit after the triply-reflected tropical sun outside.

"Skimmer?" said a man. I blinked and nodded at him. "I'm Mullane—shift assignment. I got a question to ask you, Groby." He peered at my profile card. "We need a skimmer on the sixty-seventh tier and we need a skimmer on the forty-first tier. Your bunk's going to be on the forty-third tier of the pylon. Frankly, which would you rather work on? I ought to mention that we don't have elevators for skimmers and the other Class 2 people."

"The forty-first-tier job," I told him, trying to make out his face.

"That's very sensible," he told me. "Very, very sensible." And then he just stood there, with seconds ticking away. At last he added: "I like to see a sensible man act sensible." There was another long pause.

"I haven't got any money on me," I told him.

"That's all right," he said. "I'll lend you some. Just sign this note and we can settle up on payday without any fuss. It's just a simple assignment of five dollars."

I read the note and signed it. I had to look at my profile card again; I had forgotten my first name. Mullane briskly scrawled "41" and his initials on my assignment, and hurried off without lending me five dollars. I didn't chase him.

"I'm Mrs. Horrocks, the housing officer," a woman said sweetly to me. "Welcome to the Chlorella family, Mr. Groby. I hope you'll spend many happy years with us. And now to work. Mr. Mullane told you this draft of crumbs—that is, the present group of contractees—will be housed on the forty-third tier, I think. It's my job to see that you're located with a congenial group of fellow-employees."

Her face reminded me faintly of a tarantula as she went on: "We have one vacant bunk in Dorm Seven. Lots of *nice, young* men in Dorm Seven. Perhaps you'd like it there. It means so much to be among one's *own kind* of people."

I got what she was driving at and told her I didn't want to be in Dorm Seven.

She went on brightly: "Then there's Dorm Twelve. It's a rather rough crowd, I'm afraid, but beggars can't be choosers, can they? They'd like to get a nice young man like you in Dorm Twelve. My, yes! But you could carry a knife or something. Shall I put you down for Dorm Twelve, Mr. Groby?"

"No," I said. "What else have you got? And by the way, I wonder if you could lend me five dollars until payday?"

"I'll put you down for Dorm Ten," she said, scribbling. "And of course I'll lend you some money. Ten dollars? Just sign and thumbprint this assignment, Mr. Groby. Thank you." She hurried off in search of the next sucker.

A red-faced fat man gripped my hand and said hoarsely: "Brother, I want to welcome you to the ranks of the United Slime-Mold Protein Workers of Panamerica, Unaffiliated, Chlorella Costa Rica Local. This pamphlet will explain how the U.S.M.P.W.P. protects workers in the field from the innumable petty rackets and abuses that useta plague the innustry. Yet inishiashun and dues are checked off automatically but this valable pamphlet is an extra."

I asked him: "Brother, what's the worst that can happen to me if I don't buy it?"

"It's a long drop," he said simply.

He lent me five dollars to buy the pamphlet.

I didn't have to climb to Dorm Ten on the forty-third tier. There were no elevators for Class 2 people, but there was an endless cargo net we could grab hold of. It took a little daring to jump on and off, and clearance was negligible. If your rump stuck out you were likely to lose it.

The dorm was jammed with about sixty bunks, three high. Since production went on only during the daylight hours, the hotbed system wasn't in use. My bunk was all mine, twenty-four hours a day. Big deal.

A sour-faced old man was sweeping the central aisle lackadaisically when I came in. "You a new crumb?" he asked, and looked at my ticket. "There's your bunk. I'm Pine. Room orderly. You know how to skim?"

"No," I said. "Look, Mr. Pine, how do I make a phone call out of here?"

"Dayroom," he said, jerking his thumb. I went to the dayroom adjoining. There was a phone and a biggish hypnoteleset and readers and spools and magazines. I ground my teeth as the cover of *Taunton's Weekly* sparkled at me from the rack. The phone was a pay phone, of course.

I dashed back into the dorm. "Mr. Pine," I said, "can you lend me about twenty dollars in coin? I have to make a long-distance call."

"Twenty-five for twenty?" he asked shrewdly.

"Sure. Anything you say."

He slowly scrawled out an assignment slip and I signed and printed it. Then he carefully counted out the money from his baggy pockets.

I wanted to call Kathy, but didn't dare. She might be at her apartment, she might be at the hospital. I might miss her. I dialed the fifteen digits of the Fowler Schocken Associates number after I deposited a clanging stream of coins. I waited for the switchboard to say: "Fowler Schocken Associates; good afternoon; it's *always* a good afternoon for Fowler Schocken Associates and their clients. May I help you?"

But that isn't what I heard. The phone said: *"Su número de prioridad, por favor?"*

Priority number for long-distance calls. I didn't have one. A firm had to be rated a billion and fast

90

pay before it could get a long-distance priority number in four figures. So jammed were the world's long lines that an individual priority in any number of figures was unthinkable. Naturally all that had never worried me when I made long-distance calls from Fowler Schocken, on the Fowler Schocken priority number. A priority number was one of the little luxuries I'd have to learn to live without.

I hung up slowly. The coins were not returned.

I could write to everybody, I thought. Write to Kathy and Jack O'Shea and Fowler and Collier and Hester and Tildy. Leave no stone unturned. Dear Wife (or Boss): This is to advise you that your husband (or employee) who you know quite well is dead is not really dead but inexplicably a contract laborer for Costa Rican Chlorella and please drop everything and get him out. Signed, your loving husband (or employee), Mitchell Courtenay.

But there was the company censor to think of.

I wandered blankly back into the dorm. The rest of the Dorm Ten people were beginning to drift in.

"A crumb!" one of them yelled, sighting me.

"Court's called to order!" another one trumpeted.

I don't hold what followed against any of them. It was traditional, a break in the monotony, a chance to lord it over somebody more miserable than themselves, something they had all gone through too. I presume that in Dorm Seven it would have been a memorably nasty experience, and in Dorm Twelve I might not have lived through it. Dorm Ten was just high-spirited. I paid my "fine"—more pay vouchers—and took my lumps and recited the blasphemous oath and then I was a full-fledged member of the dorm.

I didn't troop with them to the mess hall for dinner. I just lay on my bunk and wished I were as dead as the rest of the world thought I was.

8

SCUM-SKIMMING
wasn't hard to learn. You got up at dawn. You gulped a breakfast sliced not long ago from Chicken Little and washed it down with Coffiest. You put on your coveralls and took the cargo net up to your tier. In blazing noon from sunrise to sunset you walked your acres of shallow tanks crusted with algae. If you walked slowly, every thirty seconds or so you spotted a patch at maturity, bursting with yummy carbohydrates. You skimmed the patch with your skimmer and slung it down the well, where it would be baled, or processed into glucose to feed Chicken Little, who would be sliced and packed to feed people from Baffinland to Little America. Every hour you could drink from your canteen and take a salt tablet. Every two hours you could take five minutes.

At sunset you turned in your coveralls and went to dinner—more slices from Chicken Little—and then you were on your own. You could talk, you could read, you could go into trance before the dayroom hypnoteleset, you could shop, you could pick fights, you could drive yourself crazy thinking of what might have been, you could go to sleep.

Mostly you went to sleep.

I wrote a lot of letters and tried to sleep a lot. Payday came as a surprise. I didn't know two weeks had slipped by. It left me owing Chlorella Proteins only eighty-odd dollars and a few cents. Besides the various assignments I had made, there were the Employee Welfare Fund (as closely as I could figure that one out, it meant that I was paying Chlorella's taxes); union dues and installment on the initiation fee; withholding tax (this time my own taxes); hospitalization (but try and get it, the older men said) and old age insurance.

One of the things I faintheartedly consoled myself with was the thought that when—*when,* I always said firmly—I got out I'd be closer to the consumers than any ad man in the profession. Of course at Fowler Schocken we'd had our boys up from the ranks: scholarship kids. I knew now that they had been too snobbish to give me the straight facts on consumers' lives and thoughts. Or they hadn't cared to admit even to themselves what they had been like.

I think I learned that ads work more strongly on the unconscious than even we in the profession had thought. I was shocked repeatedly to hear advertising referred to as "that crap." I was at first puzzled and then gratified to see it sink in and take effect anyway. The Venus-rocket response was, of course, my greatest interest. For one week I listened when I could to enthusiasm growing among these men who would never go to Venus, who knew nobody who would ever go to Venus. I heard the limericks we had launched from Fowler Schocken Associates chuckled over:

A midget space-jock named O'Shea
Loved a girl who was built like a dray—

Or:

A socially misfit machinist
Asked his sweetheart: "Dear, what's come be-
tween us?"

Or any of the others, with their engineered-in message: that Venus environment increased male potency. Ben Winston's subsection on Folkways, I had always said, was one of the most important talent groups in the whole Schocken enterprise. They were particularly fine on riddles: "Why do they call Venus the Mourning Star?", for instance. Well, it doesn't make sense in print; but the pun is basic humor, and the basic drive of the human race is sex. And what is, essentially, more important in life than to mold and channel the deepest torrential flow of human emotion into its proper directions? (I am not apologizing for those renegades who talk fancifully about some imagined "Death-Wish" to hook their sales appeals to. I leave that sort of thing to the Tauntons of our profession; it's dirty, it's immoral, I want nothing to do with it. Besides, it leads to fewer consumers in the long run, if they'd only think the thing through.)

For there is no doubt that linking a sales message to one of the great prime motivations of the human spirit does more than sell goods; it strengthens the motivation, helps it come to the surface, provides it with focus. And thus we are assured of the steady annual increment of consumers so essential to expansion.

Chlorella, I was pleased to learn, took extremely good care of its workers' welfare in that respect. There was an adequate hormone component in the diet, and a splendid thousand-bed Recreation Room on the 50th tier. The only stipulation the company made was that children born on the plantation were automatically indentured to Chlorella if either parent was still an employee on the child's tenth birthday.

But I had no time for the Recreation Room. I was learning the ropes, studying my milieu, waiting for opportunity to come. If opportunity didn't come soon I would make opportunity; but first I had to study and learn.

Meanwhile, I kept my ears open for the results of the Venus campaign. It went beautifully—for a while. The limericks, the planted magazine stories, the gay little songs had their effect.

Then something went sour.

There was a downtrend. It took me a day to notice it, and a week to believe it could be true. The word "Venus" drifted out of the small talk. When the space rocket was mentioned it was in connection with reference points like "radiation poisoning," "taxes," "sacrifice." There was a new, dangerous kind of Folkways material—"Didja hear the one about the punchy that got caught in his space suit?"

You might not have recognized what was going on, and Fowler Schocken, scanning his daily precis of the summary of the digests of the skeletonized reports of the abstracts of the charts of progress on Venus Project, would never have the chance to question or doubt what was told him. But I knew Venus Project. And I knew what was happening.

Matt Runstead had taken over.

The aristocrat of Dorm Ten was Herrera. After ten years with Chlorella he had worked his way up—topographically it was down—to Master Slicer. He worked in the great, cool vault underground, where Chicken Little grew and was cropped by him and other artisans. He swung a sort of two-handed sword that carved off great slabs of the tissue, leaving it to the lesser packers and trimmers and their faceless helpers to weigh it, shape it, freeze it, cook it, flavor it, package it, and ship it off to the area on quota for the day.

He had more than a production job. He was a safety valve. Chicken Little grew and grew, as she had been growing for decades. Since she had started as a lump of heart tissue, she didn't know any better than to grow up against a foreign body and surround it. She didn't know any better than to grow and fill her concrete vault and keep growing, compressing her cells and rupturing them. As long as she got nutrient, she grew. Herrera saw to it that she grew round and plump, that no tissue got old and tough before it was sliced, that one side was not neglected for the other.

With this responsibility went commensurate pay, and yet Herrera had not taken a wife or an apartment in one of the upper tiers of the pylon. He made trips that were the subject of bawdy debate while he was gone—and which were never referred to without careful politeness while he was present. He kept his two-handed slicer by him at all times, and often idly sleeked its edge with a hone. He was a man I had to know. He was a man with money—he *must* have money after ten years—and I needed it.

The pattern of the B labor contract had become quite clear. You never got out of debt. Easy credit was part of the system, and so were irritants that forced you to exercise it. If I fell behind ten dollars a week I would owe one thousand one hundred dollars to Chlorella at the end of my contract, and would have to work until the debt was wiped out. And while I worked, a new debt would accumulate.

I needed Herrera's money to buy my way out of Chlorella and back to New York: Kathy, my wife; Venus Section, my job. Runstead was doing things I didn't like to Venus Section. And God alone knew what Kathy was doing, under the impression that she was a widow. I tried not to think of one particular thing: Jack O'Shea and Kathy. The little man had been getting back at womankind for their years of contempt. Until the age of twenty-five he had been a laughable sixty-pound midget, with a touch of grotesquerie in the fact that he had doggedly made himself a test pilot. At the age of twenty-six he found himself the world's number one celebrity, the first man to land a ship on Venus, an immortal barely out of his teens. He had a lot of loving to catch up on. The story was that he'd been setting records on his lecture tours. I didn't like the story. I didn't like the way he liked Kathy or the way Kathy liked him.

And so I went through another day, up at dawn, breakfast, coveralls and goggles, cargo net, skimming and slinging for blazing hour after hour, dinner and the dayroom and, if I could manage it, a chat with Herrera.

"Fine edge on that slicer, Gus. There's only two kinds of people in the world: the ones who don't take care of their tools and the smart ones."

Suspicious look from under his Aztec brows. "Pays to do things right. You're the crumb, ain't you?"

"Yeah. First time here. Think I ought to stay?"

He didn't get it. "You *gotta* stay. Contract." And he went to the magazine rack.

Tomorrow's another day.

"Hello, Gus. Tired?"

"Hi, George. Yeah, a little. Ten hours swinging the slicer. It gets you in the arms."

"I can imagine. Skimming's easy, but you don't need brains for it."

"Well, maybe some day you get upgraded. I think I'll trance."

And another:

"Hi, George. How's it going?"

"Can't complain, Gus. At least I'm getting a sun-tan."

"You sure are. Soon you be dark like me. Haw-haw! How'd you like that?"

"Porque no, amigo?"

"Hey, *tu hablas español! Cuando aprendiste la lengua?"*

"Not so fast, Gus! Just a few words here and there. I wish I knew more. Some day when I get a few bucks ahead I'm going to town and see the girls."

"Oh, they all speak English, kind of. If you get a nice steady li'l girl it would be nice to speak a li'l Spanish. She would appreciate it. But most of them know 'Gimmy-gimmy' and the li'l English

poem about what you get for one buck. Haw-
haw!"

And another day—an astonishing day.

I'd been paid again, and my debt had increased
by eight dollars. I'd tormented myself by wondering where the money went, but I knew. I
came off shift dehydrated, as they wanted me to
be. I got a squirt of Popsie from the fountain by
punching my combination—twenty-five cents
checked off my payroll. The squirt wasn't quite
enough so I had another—fifty cents. Dinner was
drab as usual; I couldn't face more than a bite or
two of Chicken Little. Later I was hungry and
there was the canteen where I got Crunchies on
easy credit. The Crunchies kicked off withdrawal
symptoms that could be quelled only by another
two squirts of Popsie from the fountain. And Popsie kicked off withdrawal symptoms that could
only be quelled by smoking Starr Cigarettes, which
made you hungry for Crunchies . . . Had Fowler
Schocken thought of it in these terms when he
organized Starrzelius Verily, the first spherical
trust? Popsie to Crunchies to Starrs to Popsie?

And you paid 6 per cent interest on the money
advanced you.

It had to be soon. If I didn't get out soon I
never would. I could feel my initiative, the thing
that made me *me* dying, cell by cell, within me.
The minute dosages of alkaloid were sapping my
will, but most of all it was a hopeless, trapped
feeling that things were this way, that they always
would be this way, that it wasn't too bad, that you
could always go into trance or get really lit on
Popsie or maybe try one of the green capsules
that floated around from hand to hand at varying

quotations; the boys would be glad to wait for the money.

It had to be soon.

"Como 'sta, Gustavo?"

He sat down and gave me his Aztec grin. *"Como 'sta, amigo Jorge? Se fuma?"* He extended a pack of cigarettes.

They were Greentips. I said automatically: "No thanks. I smoke Starrs; they're tastier." And automatically I lit one, of course. I was becoming the kind of consumer we used to love. Think about smoking, think about Starrs, light a Starr. Light a Starr, think about Popsie, get a squirt. Get a squirt, think about Crunchies, buy a box. Buy a box, think about smoking, light a Starr. And at every step roll out the words of praise that had been dinned into you through your eyes and ears and pores.

"I smoke Starrs; they're tastier. I drink Popsie; it's zippy. I eat Crunchies; they tang your tongue. I smoke—"

Gus said to me: "You don't look so happy, Jorge."

"I don't feel so happy, amigo." This was it. "I'm in a very strange situation." Wait for him, now.

"I figured there was something wrong. An intelligent fellow like you, a fellow who's been around. Maybe you can use some help?"

Wonderful; wonderful. "You won't lose by it, Gus. You're taking a chance, but you won't lose by it. Here's the story—"

"Sst! Not here!" he shushed me. In a lower voice he went on: "It's always a risk. It's always worth it when I see a smart young fellow wise up and begin to *do* things. Some day I make a mistake, *seguro*. Then they get me, maybe they brainburn me. What the hell, I can laugh at them. I done my part. Here. I don't have to tell you to be careful where you open this." He shook my hand and I felt a wad of something adhere to my palm. Then he strolled across the dayroom to the hypnoteleset, punched his clock number for a half-hour of trance and slid under, with the rest of the viewers.

I went to the washroom and punched my combination for a ten-minute occupancy of a booth—bang went another nickel off my pay—and went in. The adhesive wad on my palm opened up into a single sheet of tissue paper which said:

A Life Is In Your Hands

This is Contact Sheet One of the World Conservationist Association, popularly known as "The Consies." It has been passed to you by a member of the W.C.A. who judged that you are (a) intelligent; (b) disturbed by the present state of the world; (c) a potentially valuable addition to our ranks. His life is now in your hands. We ask you to read on before you take any action.

Facts About the W.C.A.

The Facts: The W.C.A. is a secret organization persecuted by all the governments of the world. It believes that reckless exploitation of natural resources has created needless poverty and needless human misery. It believes that continued exploitation will mean the end of human life on Earth. It believes that this trend may be reversed if the people of the Earth can be educated to the point where they will demand planning of population, reforestation, soil-building, deurbanization, and an end to the wasteful production of gadgets and proprietary foods for which there is no natural demand. This educational program is being carried on by propaganda—like this—demonstrations of force, and sabotage of factories which produce trivia.

Falsehoods About the W.C.A.

You have probably heard that "the Consies" are murderers, psychotics, and incompetent people who kill and destroy for irrational ends or out of envy. None of this is true. W.C.A. members are humane, balanced persons, many of them successful in the eyes of the world. Stories to the contrary are zealously encouraged by people who profit from the exploitation which we hope to correct. There are irrational, unbalanced and criminal persons who do commit outrages in the name of conservation, either idealistically or as a shield for looting. The W.C.A. dissociates itself from such people and regards their activities with repugnance.

What Will You Do Next?

That is up to you. You can (a) denounce the person who passed you this contact sheet; (b) destroy this sheet and forget about it; (c) go to the person who passed you the sheet and seek further information. We ask you to think before you act.

I thought—hard. I thought the broadside was (a) the dullest, lousiest piece of copysmithing I had ever seen in my life; (b) a wildly distorted version of reality; (c) a possible escape route for me out of Chlorella and back to Kathy.

So these were the dreaded Consies! Of all the

self-contradictory gibberish—but it had a certain appeal. The ad was crafted—unconsciously, I was sure—he way we'd do a pharmaceutical-house booklet for doctors only. Calm, learned, we're all men of sound judgment and deep scholarship here; we can talk frankly about bedrock issues. Does your patient suffer from hyperspasm, Doctor?

It was an appeal to reason, and they're always dangerous. You can't trust reason. We threw it out of the ad profession long ago and have never missed it.

Well; there were obviously two ways to do it. I could go to the front office and put the finger on Herrera. I'd get a little publicity maybe; they'd listen to me, maybe; they *might* believe enough of what I told them to check. I seemed to recall that denouncers of Consies were sometimes brain-burned on the sensible grounds that they had been exposed to the virus and that it might work out later, after the first healthy reaction. That wasn't good. Riskier but more heroic: I could bore from within, playing along with the Consies. If they were the world-wide net they claimed to be, there was no reason why I shouldn't wind up in New York, ready and able to blow the lid off them.

Not for a moment did I have any doubts about being able to get ahead. My fingers itched for a pencil to mark up that contact sheet, sharpening the phrases, cutting out the dullness, inserting see-hear-taste-feel words with real shock. It could use it.

The door of the booth sprang open; my ten minutes were up. I hastily flushed the contact sheet down the drain and went out into the day room. Herrera was still in the trance before the set.

I waited some twenty minutes. Finally he shook himself, blinked, and looked around. He saw me, and his face was immobile granite. I smiled and nodded, and he came over. "All right, *compañero?*" he asked quietly.

"All right," I said. "Any time you say, Gus."

"It will be soon," he said. "Always after a thing like that I plug in for some trance. I cannot stand the suspense of waiting to find out. Some day I come up out of trance and find the bulls are beating hell out of me, eh?" He began to sleek the edge of his slicer with the pocket hone.

I looked at it with new understanding. "For the bulls?" I asked.

His face was shocked. "No," he said. "You have the wrong idea a little, Jorge. For me. So I have no chance to rat."

His words were noble, even in such a cause. I hated the twisted minds who had done such a thing to a fine consumer like Gus. It was something like murder. He could have played his part in the world, buying and using and making work and profits for his brothers all around the globe, ever increasing his wants and needs, ever increasing everybody's work and profits in the circle of consumption, raising children to be consumers in turn. It hurt to see him perverted into a sterile zealot.

I resolved to do what I could for him when I blew off the lid. The fault did not lie with him. It was the people who had soured him on the world who should pay. Surely there must be some sort of remedial treatment for Consies like Gus who were only dupes. I would ask—no; it would be better not to ask. People would jump to conclusions. I could hear them now: "I don't say Mitch isn't sound, but it was a pretty far-fetched idea." "Yeah. Once a Consie, always a Consie." "Everybody knows that. I don't say Mitch isn't sound, mind you, but—"

The hell with Herrera. He could take his chances like everybody else. Anybody who sets out to turn the world upside down has no right to complain if he gets caught in its gears.

9

DAYS WENT BY like weeks. Herrera talked little to me, until one evening in the dayroom he suddenly asked: "You ever see *Gallina?*" That was Chicken Little. I said no. "Come on down, then. I can get you in. She's a sight."

We walked through corridors and leaped for the descending cargo net. I resolutely shut my eyes. You look straight down that thing and you get the high-shy horrors. Forty, Thirty, Twenty, Ten, Zero, Minus Ten—

"Jump off, Jorge," Herrera said. "Below Minus Ten is the machinery." I jumped.

Minus Ten was gloomy and sweated water from its concrete walls. The roof was supported by immense beams. A tangle of pipes jammed the corridor where we got off. "Nutrient fluid," Herrera said.

I asked about the apparently immense weight of the ceiling. "Concrete and lead. It shields cosmic rays. Sometimes a *Gallina* goes cancer." He spat. "No good to eat for people. You got to burn it all if you don't catch it real fast and—" He swung his glittering slicer in a screaming arc to show me what he meant by "catch."

He swung open a door. "This is her nest," he said proudly. I looked and gulped.

It was a great concrete dome, concrete-floored. Chicken Little filled most of it. She was a gray-brown, rubbery hemisphere some fifteen yards in diameter. Dozens of pipes ran into her pulsating flesh. You could see that she was alive.

Herrera said to me: "All day I walk around her. I see a part growing fast, it looks good and tender, I slice." His two-handed blade screamed again. This time it shaved off an inch-thick Chicken Little steak. "Crumbs behind me hook it away and cut it up and put it on the conveyor." There were tunnel openings spotted around the circumference of the dome, with idle conveyor belts visible in them.

"Doesn't she grow at night?"

"No. They turn down the nutrient just enough, they let the waste accumulate in her just right. Each night she almost dies. Each morning she comes to life like San Lázaro. But nobody ever pray before *pobrecita Gallina,* hey?" He whacked the rubbery thing affectionately with the flat of his slicer.

"You like her," I said inanely.

"Sure, Jorge. She does tricks for me." He looked around and then marched the circuit of the nest, peering into each of the tunnel mouths. Then he took a short beam from one of them and casually braced it against the door to the nest. It fitted against a cross-bar on the door and against a seemingly-random groove in the concrete floor. It would do very well as a lock.

"I'll show you the trick," he said, with an Aztec grin. With a magician's elaborate gesture he took from his pocket a sort of whistle. It didn't have a mouthpiece. It had an air tank fed by a small hand pump. "I didn't make this," he hastened to assure me. "They call it Galton's whistle, but who this Galton is I don't know. Watch—and listen."

He began working the pump, pointing the whistle purposefully at Chicken Little. I heard no sound, but I shuddered as the rubbery protoplasm bulged in away from the pipe in the hemispherical depression.

"Don't be scared, *compañero*," he told me. "Just follow." He pumped harder and passed me a flashlight which I stupidly turned on. Herrera played the soundless blast of the whistle against Chicken Little like a hose. She reacted with a bigger and bigger cavity that finally became an archway whose floor was the concrete floor of the nest.

Herrera walked into the archway, saying: "Follow." I did, my heart pounding frightfully. He inched forward, pumping the whistle, and the archway became a dome. The entrance into Chicken Little behind us became smaller . . . smaller . . . smaller . . .

We were quite inside, in a hemispherical bubble moving slowly through a hundred-ton lump of gray-brown, rubbery flesh. "Light on the floor, *compañero,*" he said, and I flashed it on the floor. The concrete was marked with lines that looked accidental, but which guided Herrera's feet. We inched forward, and I wondered vividly what would happen if the Galton whistle sprang a leak . . .

After about two thousand years of inch-by-inch progress my light flashed on a crescent of metal. Herrera piped the bubble over it, and it became a disk. Still pumping, he stamped three times on it. It flipped open like a manhole. "You first," he said, and I dived into it, not knowing or caring whether the landing would be hard or soft. It was soft, and I lay there, shuddering. A moment later Herrera landed beside me and the manhole above clapped shut. He stood up, massaging his arm. "Hard work," he said. "I pump and pump that thing and I don't hear it. Some day it's going to stop working and I won't know the difference until—" He grinned again.

"George Groby," Herrera introduced me. "This is Ronnie Bowen." He was a short, phlegmatic consumer in a front-office suit. "And this is Arturo Denzer." Denzer was very young and nervous.

The place was a well-lighted little office, all concrete, with air regenerators. There were desks and communication equipment. It was hard to believe that the only way to get in was barred by that mountain of protoplasm above. It was harder to believe that the squeak of inaudibly high-frequency sound waves could goad that insensate hulk into moving aside.

Bowen took over. "Pleased to have you with us, Groby," he said. "Herrera says you have brains. We don't go in a great deal for red tape, but I want your profile."

I gave him Groby's profile and he took it down. His mouth tightened with suspicion as I told him the low educational level. "I'll be frank," he said. "You don't talk like an uneducated man."

"You know how some kids are," I said. "I spent my time reading and viewing. It's tough being right in the middle of a family of five. You aren't old enough to be respected and you aren't young enough to be the pet. I felt kind of lost and I kept trying to better myself."

He accepted it. "Fair enough. Now, what can you do?"

"Well . . . I think I can write a better contact sheet than you use."

"Indeed. What else?"

"Well, propaganda generally. You could start stories going around and people wouldn't know they were from the Co—from us. Things to make them feel discontented and wake them up."

"That's a very interesting idea. Give me an example."

My brain was chugging nicely. "Start a rumor going around the mess hall that they've got a way of making new protein. Say it tastes exactly like roast beef and you'll be able to buy it at a dollar a pound. Say it's going to be announced in three days. Then when the three days are up and there's no announcement start a wisecrack going. Like: 'What's the difference between roast beef and Chicken Little?' Answer, 'A hundred and fifty years of progress.' Something like that catches on

109

and it'll make them think about the old days favorably."

It was easy. It wasn't the first time I'd turned my talent to backing a product I didn't care for personally.

Bowen was taking it down on a silenced typewriter. "Good," he said. "Very ingenious, Groby. We'll try that. Why do you say 'three days'?"

I couldn't very well tell him that three days was the optimum priming period for a closed social circuit to be triggered with a catalytic cue-phrase, which was the book answer. I said instead, with embarrassment: "It just seemed about right to me."

"Well, we'll try it at that. Now, Groby, you're going to have a study period. We've got the classic conservationist texts, and you should read them. We've got special publications of interest to us which you should follow: *Statistical Abstracts, Journal of Space Flight, Biometrika, Agricultural Bulletin,* and lots more. If you run into tough going, and I expect you will, ask for help. Eventually you should pick a subject to which you're attracted and specialize in it, with an eye to research. An informed conservationist is an effective conservationist."

"Why the *Journal of Space Flight?*" I asked, with a growing excitement. Suddenly there seemed to be an answer: Runstead's sabotage, my kidnaping, the infinite delays and breakdowns in the project. Were they Consie plots? Could the Consies, in their depraved, illogical minds, have decided that space travel was antisurvival, or whatever you call it?

"Very important," said Bowen. "You need to know all you can about it."

I probed. "You mean so we can louse it up?"

"Of course not!" Bowen exploded. "Good God, Groby, think what Venus means to us—an unspoiled planet, all the wealth the race needs, all the fields and food and raw materials. Use your head, man!"

"Oh," I said. The Gordian knot remained unslashed.

I curled up with the reels of *Biometrika* and every once in a while asked for an explanation which I didn't need. *Biometrika* was one of the everyday tools of a copysmith. It told the story of population changes, IQ changes, death rate and causes of death, and all the rest of it. Almost every issue had good news in it for us—the same news that these Consies tut-tutted over. Increase of population was always good news to us. More people, more sales. Decrease of IQ was always good news to us. Less brains, more sales. But these eccentrically-oriented fanatics couldn't see it that way, and I had to pretend to go along with them.

I switched to the *Journal of Space Flight* after a while. There the news was bad—*all* bad. There was public apathy; there was sullen resistance to the shortages that the Venus rocket construction entailed; there was defeatism about planting a Venus colony at all; there was doubt that the colony could do anything if it ever did get planted.

That damned Runstead!

But the worst news of all was on the cover of the latest issue. The cutline said: "Jack O'Shea Grins As Pretty Friend Congratulates With Kiss After President Awards Medal Of Honor." The pretty friend was my wife Kathy. She never looked lovelier.

I got behind the Consie cell and pushed. In three days there was a kind of bubbling discontent about the mess hall chow. In a week the consumers were saying things like: "I wish to hell I was born a hundred years ago . . . I wish to hell this dorm wasn't so God-damned crowded . . . I wish to hell I could get out on a piece of land somewheres and work for myself."

The minute cell was elated. Apparently I had done more in a week than they had done in a year. Bowen—he was in Personnel—told me: "We need a head like yours, Groby. You're not going to sweat your life away as a scum-skimmer. One of these days the assignment boss will ask you if you know nutrient chemistry. Tell him 'Yes.' I'll give you a quickie course in everything you need to know. We'll get you out of the hot sun yet."

It happened in another week, when everybody was saying things like: "Be nice to walk in a forest some day. Can y'imagine all those trees they useta have?" and: "God-damn salt-water soap!" when it had never before occurred to them to think of it as "salt-water soap." The assignment boss came up to me and duly said: "Groby! You know any nutrient chemistry?"

"Funny you should ask," I told him. "I've studied it quite a bit. I know the sulfur-phosphorus-carbon-oxygen-hydrogen-nitrogen ratios for chlorella, I know the optimum temperatures and stuff like that."

Obviously this little was much more than he knew. He grunted, "Yeah?" and went away, impressed.

A week later everybody was telling a dirty joke about the Starrzelius Verily trust and I was transferred to an eight-hour job inside the pylon, reading gauges and twisting valves that controlled the nutrient flow to the tanks of chlorella. It was lighter and easier work. I spent my time under Chicken Little—I could pass through her with a Galton whistle almost without cringing—rewriting the Consies' fantastically inept Contact Sheet One:

CAN YOU QUALIFY FOR *TOP-LEVEL* PROMOTION?

You and *only you* can answer these important questions:

Are you an intelligent, forward-looking man or woman between the ages of 14 and 50— Do you have the drive and ambition needed to handle the really BIG JOBS tomorrow will bring— Can you be trusted—*absolutely trusted* —with the biggest, hopefulest news of our time?

If you can't stand up and shout YES! to *every one* of these questions, please read no further!

But if you *can,* then you and your friends or family can get in on the *ground floor* of. . . .

And so on. Bowen was staggered. "You don't think that appeal to upper-level IQs limits it too much, do you?" he asked anxiously. I didn't tell him that the only difference between that and the standard come-on for Class 12 laborers was that the Class 12s got it aurally—they couldn't read. I said I didn't think so. He nodded. "You're a natural-born copysmith, Groby," he told me solemnly. "In a Conservationist America, you'd be star class." I was properly modest. He went on,

"I can't hog you; I've got to pass you on to a higher echelon. It isn't right to waste your talents in a cell. I've forwarded a report on you——" he gestured at the communicator, "and I expect you'll be requisitioned. It's only right. But I hate to see you go. However, I'm pulling the strings already. Here's the Chlorella Purchasers' Handbook . . ."

My heart bounded. I knew that Chlorella contracted for raw materials with a number of outlets in New York City.

"Thanks," I mumbled. "I want to serve wherever I best can."

"I know you do, Groby," he soothed. "Uh—say, one thing before you go. This isn't official, George, but—well, I do a little writing too. I've got some of my things here—sketches, I guess you'd call them—and I'd appreciate it a lot if you'd take them along and . . ."

I finally got out with the handbook, and only fourteen of Bowen's "sketches." They were churlish little scraps of writing, with no sell in them at all that I could see. Bowen assured me he had lots more that he and I could work on.

I hit that handbook hard.

Twisting valves left me feeling more alive at the end of a day than scum-skimming, and Bowen made sure my Consie labors were as light as possible—to free me for work on his "sketches." The result was that, for the first time, I had leisure to explore my milieu. Herrera took me into town with him once, and I discovered what he did with those unmentioned week ends. The knowledge shocked, but did not disgust me. If anything, it reminded me that the gap between executive and consumer could not be bridged by anything as abstract and unreal as "friendship."

Stepping out of the old-fashioned pneumatic tube into a misty Costa Rican drizzle, we stopped first at a third-rate restaurant for a meal. Herrera insisted on getting us each a potato, and insisted on being allowed to pay for it—"No, Jorge, you call it a celebration. You let me go on living after I gave you the contact sheet, no? So we celebrate." Herrera was brilliant through the meal, a fountain of conversation and bilingual badinage with me and the waiters. The sparkle in his eye, the rapid, compulsive flow of speech, the easy, unnecessary laughter were like nothing so much as the gaiety of a young man on a date.

A young man on a date. I remembered my first meeting with Kathy, that long afternoon at Central Park, strolling hand in hand down the dim-lit corridors, the dance hall, the eternal hour we stood outside her door. . . .

Herrera reached over and pounded me on the shoulder, and I saw that he and the waiter were laughing. I laughed too, defensively, and their laughter doubled; evidently the joke had been on me. "Never mind, Jorge," said Herrera, sobering, "we go now. You will like what I have for us to do next, I think." He paid the check, and the waiter raised an eyebrow.

"In back?"

"In back," said Herrera. "Come, Jorge."

We threaded our way between the counters, the waiter leading the way. He opened a door and hissed something rapid and Spanish to Herrera. "Oh, don't worry," Herrera told him. "We will not be long."

"In back," turned out to be—a library.

I was conscious of Herrera's eyes on me, and I don't think I showed any of what I felt. I even stayed with him for an hour or so, while he devoured a wormy copy of something called *Moby Dick* and I glanced through half a dozen ancient magazines. Some of those remembered classics went a long way toward easing my conscience—there was actually an early "Do You Make These Common Mistakes in English?" and a very fine "Not a Cough in a Carload" that would have looked well on the wall of my office, back in Schocken Tower. But I could not relax in the presence of so many books without a word of advertising in any of them. I am not a prude about solitary pleasures when they serve a useful purpose. But my tolerance has limits.

Herrera knew, I think, that I lied when I told him I had a headache. When, much later, he came stumbling into the dorm I turned my head away. We scarcely spoke after that.

A week later, after a near-riot in the mess hall —sparked by a rumor that the yeast fritters were adulterated with sawdust—I was summoned to the front office.

A veep for Personnel saw me after I had waited an hour. "Groby?"

"Yes, Mr. Milo."

"Remarkable record you've made. Quite remarkable. I see your efficiency rating is straight fours."

That was Bowen's work. He kept records. He had taken five years to worm himself into that very spot. "Thank you, Mr. Milo."

"Welcome, I'm sure. We, uh, happen to have a vacancy approaching. One of our people up North. I see his work is falling off badly."

Not his work—the ghost of his work; the shadow

on paper of his work; the shadow carefully outlined and filled in by Bowen. I began to appreciate the disproportionate power that Consies could wield.

"Do you happen to have any interest in purchasing, Groby?"

"It's odd that you should ask, Mr. Milo," I said evenly. "I've always had a feel for it. I think I'd make good in purchasing."

He looked at me skeptically; it was a pretty standard answer. He began firing questions and I respectfully regurgitated answers from the Chlorella manual. He had memorized it twenty-odd years ago, and I had memorized it only a week ago. He was no match for me. After an hour he was convinced that George Groby was the only hope of Chlorella Protein, and that I should be hurled into the breach forthwith.

That night I told the cell about it.

"It means New York," Bowen said positively. "It means New York." I couldn't keep back a great sigh. Kathy, I thought. He went on, heedlessly: "I've got to tell you some special things now. To begin with—the recognition signals."

I learned the recognition signals. There was a hand sign for short range. There was a grand hailing sign of distress for medium range. For long range there was a newspaper-ad code; quite a good one. He made me practice the signs and memorize the code cold. It took us into the small hours of the morning. When we left through Chicken Little I realized that I hadn't seen Herrera all day. I asked as we emerged what had happened.

"He broke," Bowen said simply.

I didn't say anything. It was a kind of shorthand talk among Consies. "Soandso broke." That meant: "Soandso toiled for years and years in the cause of the W.C.A. He gave up his nickels and dimes and the few pleasures they could buy him. He didn't marry and he didn't sleep with women because it would have imperiled security. He became possessed by doubts so secret that he didn't admit them to himself or us. The doubts and fears mounted. He was torn too many ways and he turned on himself and died."

"Herrera broke," I said stupidly.

"Don't brood about it," Bowen said sharply. "You're going North. You've got a job to do."

Indeed I had.

10

I WENT TO NEW York City almost respectably, in a cheap front-office suit, aboard a tourist rocket, steerage class. Above me the respectable Costa Rican consumers oohed and ahed at the view from the prism windows or anxiously counted their pennies, wondering how far they'd take them in the pleasures for sale by the colossus of the North.

Below decks we were a shabbier, tougher gang, but it was no labor freighter. We had no windows, but we had lights and vending machines and buckets. A plant protection man had made a little speech to us before we loaded: "You crumbs are going North, out of Costa Rican jurisdiction. You're going to better jobs. But don't forget that they are *jobs*. I want each and every one of you to remember that you're in hock to Chlorella and that Chlorella's claim on you is a prior lien. If any of you think you can break your contract, you're going to find out just how fast and slick extradition for a commercial offense can be. And if any of you think you can just disappear, try it. Chlorella pays Burns Detective Agency seven billion a year, and Burns delivers the goods. So if you crumbs want to give us a little easy exercise, go ahead; we'll be waiting for you. Is everything clear?" Everything was clear. "All right, crumbs. Get aboard and good luck. You have your assignment tickets. Give my regards to Broadway."

We slid into a landing at Montauk without incident. Down below, we sat and waited while the consumers on tourist deck filed out, carrying their baggage kits. Then we sat and waited while Food Customs inspectors, wearing the red-and-white A&P arm bands, argued vociferously with our stewards over the surplus rations—four of us had died on the trip, and the stewards, of course, had held out their Chicken Little cutlets to sell in the black market. Then we sat and waited.

Finally the order came to fall out in fifties. We lined up and had our wrists stamped with our entry permits; marched by squads to the subway; and entrained for the city. I had a bit of luck. My group drew a freight compartment.

At the Labor Exchange we were sorted out and tagged for our respective assignments. There was a bit of a scare when it came out that Chlorella had sold the contracts on twenty of us to I. G. Farben—nobody wants to work in the uranium mines—but I wasn't worried. The man next to me stared moodily as the guards cut out the unlucky twenty and herded them off. "Treat us like slaves," he said bitterly, plucking at my sleeve. "It's a crime. Don't you think so, Mac? It violates the essential dignity of labor."

I gave him an angry glare. The man was a Consie, pure and simple. Then I remembered that I was a Consie too, for the time being. I considered the use of the handclasp, and decided against it. He would be worth remembering if I needed help; but if I revealed myself prematurely he might call on *me*.

We moved on to the Chlorella depot in the Nyack suburbs.

Waste not, want not. Under New York, as under every city in the world, the sewage drains led to a series of settling basins and traps. I knew, as any citizen knows, how the organic waste of twenty-three million persons came water-borne through the venous tracery of the city's drains; how the salts were neutralized through ion-exchange, the residual liquid piped to the kelp farms in Long Island Sound, the sludge that remained pumped into tank barges for shipment to Chlorella. I knew about it, but I had never seen it.

My title was Procurement Expeditor, Class 9. My job was coupling the flexible hoses that handled the sludge. After the first day, I shot a week's pay on soot-extractor plugs for my nostrils; they didn't filter out all the odor, but they made it possible to live in it.

On the third day I came off shift and hit the showers. I had figured it out in advance: after six hours at the tanks, where no vending machines were for the simple reason that no one could conceivably eat, drink, or smoke *anything* in the atmosphere, the pent-up cravings of the crew kept them on the Popsie-Crunchie-Starrs cycle for half an hour before the first man even thought of a shower. By sternly repressing the craving, weaker in me than in most because it had had less time to become established, I managed to have the showers almost alone. When the mob arrived, *I* hit the vending machines. It was a simple application of intelligence, and if that doesn't bear out the essential difference between consumer and copysmith mentality, what does? Of course, as I say, the habits weren't as strong in me.

There was one other man in the shower, but, with only two of us, we hardly touched. He handed me the soap as I came in; I lathered and let the water roar down over me under the full pressure of the recirculators. I was hardly aware he was there. But, as I passed the soap back to him, I felt his third finger touch my wrist, the index finger circle around the base of my thumb.

"Oh," I said stupidly, and returned the handclasp. "Are you my con—"

"Ssh!" he hissed. He gestured irritatedly to the Muzak spy-mike dangling from the ceiling. He turned his back on me and meticulously soaped himself again.

When he returned the soap a scrap of paper clung to it. In the locker room I squeezed it dry spread it out. It read: "Tonight is pass night. Go to the Metropolitan Museum of Art, Classics Room. Be in front of the Maidenform exhibit at exactly five minutes before closing time."

I joined the queue at the supervisor's desk as soon as I was dressed. In less than half an hour I had a stamped pass authorizing me to skip bed-check for the night. I returned to my bunk to pick up my belongings, warned the new occupant of the bed about the sleep-talking of the man in the tier above, turned in my bag to the supply room, and caught the shuttle down to Bronxville. I transferred to a north-bound local, rode one station, switched to the south-bound side, and got out at Schocken Tower. No one appeared to be following me. I hadn't expected anyone to, but it never pays to take chances.

My Consie rendezvous at the Met was almost four hours off. I stood around in the lobby until a cop, contemptuously eyeing my cheap clothing, moved toward me. I had hoped Hester or perhaps even Fowler Schocken himself might come through; no such luck. I saw a good many faces I recognized, of course, but none I was sure I could trust. And, until I found out what lay behind the double cross on Starrzelius Glacier, I had no intention of telling just anybody that I was still alive.

The Pinkerton boomed, "You want to give the Schocken people your business, crumb? You got a big account for them, maybe?"

"Sorry," I said, and headed for the street door. It didn't figure that he would bother to follow me through the crowd in the lobby; he didn't. I dodged around the recreation room, where a group of consumers were watching a PregNot

122

light love story on the screen and getting their samples of Coffiest, and ducked into the service elevators. "Eightieth," I said to the operator, and at once realized I had blundered. The operator's voice said sharply through the speaker grille:

"Service elevators go only to the seventieth floor, you in Car Five. What do you want?"

"Messenger," I lied miserably. "I got to make a pickup from Mr. Schocken's office. I *told* them I wouldn't be let in to Mr. Schocken's office, a fellow like me. I told them, 'Look, he's probably got twenty-five seckataries I got to go through before they let me see him,' I said—"

"The mail room is on forty-five," the operator said, a shade less sharply. "Stand in front of the door so I can see you."

I moved into range of the ike. I didn't want to, but I couldn't see any way out. I thought I heard a sound from the grille, but there was no way of being sure. I had never been in the elevator operators' room, a thousand feet below me, where they pushed the buttons that sent the cars up and down the toothed shafts; I would have given a year's pay to have been able to look into it then.

I stood there for half a minute. Then the operator's voice said noncommittally. "All right, you. Back in the car. Forty-fifth floor, first slide to the left."

The others in the car stared at me through an incurious haze of Coffiest's alkaloids until I got out. I stepped on the leftbound slidewalk and went past the door marked "Mail Room," to the corridor juncture where my slidewalk dipped down around its roller. It took me a little while to find the stairway, but that was all right. I needed the time to catch up on my swearing. I didn't dare use the elevators again.

Have you ever climbed thirty-five flights of stairs?

Toward the end the going got pretty bad. It wasn't just that I was aching from toe to navel, or that I was wasting time, of which I had none too much anyway. It was getting on toward ten o'clock, and the consumers whose living quarters were on the stairs were beginning to drift there for the night. I was as careful as I could be, but it nearly came to a fist fight on the seventy-fourth, where the man on the third step had longer legs than I thought.

Fortunately, there were no sleepers above the seventy-eighth; I was in executive country.

I skulked along the corridors, very conscious of the fact that the first person who paid any attention to me would either recognize me or throw me out. Only clerks were in the corridors, and none I'd known at all well; my luck was running strong.

But not strong enough. Fowler Schocken's office was locked.

I ducked into the office of his secretary[3], which was deserted, and thought things over. Fowler usually played a few holes of golf at the country club after work. It was pretty late for him still to be there, but I thought I might as well take the chance—it was only four more flights to the club.

I made it standing up. The country club is a handsome layout, which is only fair because the dues are handsome too. Besides the golf links, the tennis court and the other sports facilities, the whole north end of the room is woods—more than a dozen beautifully simulated trees—and there are at least twenty recreation booths for reading, watching movies, or any other spectator pleasure.

A mixed foursome was playing golf. I moved close to their seats as unobtrusively as possible. They were intent on their dials and buttons, guiding their players along the twelfth hole fairway. I read their scores from the telltale with a sinking heart; all were in the high nineties. Duffers. Fowler Schocken averaged under eighty for the course. He couldn't be in a group like that, and as I came close I saw that both the men were strangers to me.

I hesitated before retreating, trying to decide what to do next. Schocken wasn't in sight anywhere in the club. Conceivably he was in one of the recreation booths, but I could scarcely open the doors of all of them to see; I'd be thrown out the first time I blundered into an occupied one, unless God smiled and the occupant was Fowler.

A babble of conversation from the golfers caught my ear. One of the girls had just sunk a four-inch putt to finish the hole; smiling happily as the others complimented her, she leaned forward to pull the lever that brought the puppet players back to the tee and changed the layout to the dogleg of the thirteenth hole, and I caught a glimpse of her face. It was Hester, my secretary.

That made it simple. I couldn't quite guess how Hester came to be in the country club, but I knew everything else there was to know about Hester. I retreated to an alcove near the entrance to the ladies' room; it was only about ten minutes wait before she showed up.

She fainted, of course. I swore and carried her into the alcove. There was a couch; I put her on it. There was a door; I closed it.

She blinked up at me as consciousness came back. "Mitch," she said, in a tone between a whisper and a shriek.

"I am not dead," I told her. "Somebody else died, and they switched bodies. I don't know who 'they' are; but I'm not dead. Yes, it's really me. Mitch Courtenay, your boss. I can prove it. For instance, remember last year's Christmas party, when you were so worried about—"

"Never mind," she said hastily. "My God, Mitch —I mean, Mr. Courtenay—"

"Mitch is good enough," I said. I dropped the hand I had been massaging, and she pushed herself up to get a better look at me. "Listen," I said, "I'm alive, all right, but I'm in a kind of peculiar foul-up. I've got to get in touch with Fowler Schocken. Can you fix it—right away?"

"Uh." She swallowed and reached for a cigarette, recovering. I automatically took out a Starr. "Uh, no, Mitch. Mr. Schocken's on the Moon. It's a big secret, but I guess I can tell *you* about it. It's something to do with the Venus project. After you got killed—well, you know what I mean— after that, when he put Mr. Runstead on the project and it began to slip so, he decided to take matters into his own hands. I gave him all your notes. One of them said something about the Moon, I guess; anyway, he took off a couple of days ago."

"Hell," I said. "Well, who'd he leave in charge here? Harvey Bruner? Can you reach—"

Hester was shaking her head. "No, not Mr. Bruner, Mitch. Mr. Runstead's in charge. Mr.

Schocken switched in such a hurry, there wasn't anyone to spare to take over *his* job except Mr. Runstead. But I can call him right away."

"*No,*" I said. I looked at my watch, and groaned. I would have just about time to make it to the Met. "Look," I said. "I've got to leave. Don't say anything to *anybody,* will you? I'll figure something out, and I'll call you. Let's see, when I call I'll say I'm—what's the name of that doctor of your mother's?—Dr. Gallant. And I'll arrange to meet you and tell you what we're going to do. I can count on you, Hester, can't I?"

"Sure, Mitch," she said breathlessly.

"Fine," I said. "Now you'll have to convoy me down in the elevator. I haven't got time to walk, and there'll be trouble if a guy like me gets caught on the club floor." I stopped and looked her over. "Speaking of which," I said, "what in the world are you doing here?"

Hester blushed. "Oh, you know how it is," she said unhappily. "After you were gone there weren't any other secretarial jobs; the rest of the executives had their girls, and I just couldn't be a consumer again, Mitch, not with the bills and all. And—well, there was this opening up here, you see. . . ."

"Oh," I said. I hope nothing showed on my face; God knows I tried. Damn you to hell, Runstead, I said to myself, thinking of Hester's mother and Hester's young man that she'd maybe been going to marry some day, and the absolute stinking injustice of a man like Runstead taking the law into his own hands and wrecking executive lives—mine—and staff lives—Hester's—and dragging them down to the level of consumers.

"Don't worry, Hester," I said gently. "I'll owe

you something for this. And believe me, you won't have to remind me. I'll make everything up to you." And I knew how to do it, too. Quite a lot of the girls on the ZZ contract manage to avoid the automatic renewal and downgrading. It would cost a lot for me to buy out her contract before the year was up, so that was out of the question; but some of the girls do pretty well with single executives after their first year. And I was important enough so that if I made a suggestion to some branch head or bureau chief, he would not be likely to ignore it, or even to treat her badly.

I don't approve of sentiment in business matters, but as you see I'm an absolute sucker for it in any personal relationship.

Hester insisted on lending me some money, so I made it to the Met with time to spare by taking a cab. Even though I had paid the driver in advance, he could not refrain from making a nasty comment about high-living consumers as I got out; if I hadn't had more important things on my mind I would have taught him a lesson then and there.

I have always had a fondness for the Met. I don't go much for religion—partly, I suppose, because it's a Taunton account—but there is a grave, ennobling air about the grand old masterpieces in the Met that gives me a feeling of peace and reverence. I mentioned that I was a little ahead of time. I spent those minutes standing silently before the bust of G. Washington Hill, and I felt more relaxed than I had since that first afternoon at the South Pole.

At precisely five minutes before midnight I

was standing before the big, late-period Maiden-form—number thirty-five in the catalogue: "I Dreamed I Was Ice-Fishing in My Maidenform Bra"—when I became conscious of someone whistling in the corridor behind me. The notes were irrelevant; the cadence formed one of the recognition signals I'd learned in the hidey-hole under Chicken Little.

One of the guards was strolling away. She looked over her shoulder at me and smiled.

To all external appearances, it was a casual pickup. We linked arms, and I felt the coded pressure of her fingers on my wrist: "D-O-N-T T-A-L-K W-H-E-N I L-E-A-V-E Y-O-U G-O T-O T-H-E B-A-C-K O-F T-H-E R-O-O-M S-I-T D-O-W-N A-N-D W-A-I-T."

I nodded. She took me to a plastic-finished door, pushed it open, pointed inside. I went in alone.

There were ten or fifteen consumers sitting in straight-back chairs, facing an elderly consumer with a lectorial goatee. I found a seat in the back of the room and sat in it. No one paid any particular attention to me.

The lecturer was covering the high spots of some particularly boring precommercial period. I listened with half my mind, trying to catch some point of similarity in the varying types around me. All were Consies, I was reasonably sure—else why would I be here? But the basic stigmata, the surface mark of the lurking fanatic inside, that should have been apparent, escaped me. They were all consumers, with the pinched look that soyaburgers and Yeasties inevitably give; but I could have passed any of them in the street without a second glance. Yet—this was New York, and

Bowen had spoken of it as though the Consies I'd meet here were pretty high up in the scale, the Trotskys and Tom Paines of the movement.

And that was a consideration too. When I got out of this mess—when I got through to Fowler Schocken and cleared up my status—I might be in a position to break up this whole filthy conspiracy, if I played my cards right. I looked over the persons in the room a little more attentively, memorizing their features. I didn't want to fail to recognize them, next time we came in contact.

There must have been some sort of signal, but I missed it. The lecturer stopped almost in midsentence, and a plump little man with a goatee stood up from the first row. "All right," he said in an ordinary tone, "we're all here and there's no sense wasting any more time. We're against waste; that's why we're here." He stepped on the little titter. "No noise," he warned, "and no names. For the purpose of this meeting we'll use numbers; you can call me 'One,' you 'Two'—" he pointed to the man in the next seat, "and so on by rows to the back of the room. All clear? Okay, now listen closely. We've got you together because you're all new here. You're in the big leagues now. This is world operational headquarters, right here in New York; you can't go any higher. Each of you was picked for some special quality—you know what they are. You'll all get assignments right here, tonight. But before you do, I want to point out one thing. You don't know me and I don't know you; every one of you got a big buildup from your last cells, but sometimes the men in the field get a little too enthusiastic. If they were wrong about you. . . . Well, you understand these things, eh?"

There was a general nod. I nodded too, but I paid particular attention to memorizing that plump little goatee. One by one numbers were called, and one by one the new-johns got up, conferred briefly with the goatee, and left, in couples and threes, for unannounced destinations. I was almost the last to be called; besides me, only a very young girl with orange hair and a cast in her eye was still in the room.

"Okay, you two," said the man with the goatee. "You two are going to be a team, so you might as well know names. Groby, meet Corwin. Groby's a kind of copysmith. Celia's an artist."

"Okay," she said, lighting a Starr from the butt of another in a flare of phosphorus. A perfect consumer type if only she hadn't been corrupted by these zealots; I noticed her jaws working on gum even while she chain-smoked.

"We'll get along fine," I said approvingly.

"You sure will," said the man in the goatee. "You have to. You understand these things, Groby. In order to give you a chance to show your stuff, we'll have to let you know a lot of stuff that we don't want to read in the morning paper. If you don't work out for us, Groby," he said pleasantly, "you see the fix we're in; we'll have to make some other arrangements for you." He tapped a little bottle of colorless fluid on the desk top. The tinny rattle of the aluminum top was no tinnier than my voice as I said, "Yes, sir," because I knew what little bottles of colorless fluid could reasonably be assumed to contain.

It turned out, though, that it wasn't much of a problem. I spent three difficult hours in that little room, then I pointed out that if I didn't get back to barracks I would miss the morning work call

131

and there would be hell to pay. So they excused me.

But I missed work call anyhow. I came out of the Museum into a perfect spring dawn, feeling, all in all, pretty content with life. A figure loomed out of the smog and peered into my face. I recognized the sneering face of the taxi-runner who had brought me to the Museum. He said briskly, "Hel-lo, Mr. Courtenay," and then the obelisk from behind the Museum, or something very much like it, smacked me across the back of the neck.

11

"—AWAKE IN A few minutes," I heard somebody say.

"Is he ready for Hedy?"

"Good God, no!"

"I was only asking."

"You ought to know better. First you give them amphetamine, plasma, maybe a niacin megaunit. *Then* they're ready for Hedy. She doesn't like it if they keep blacking out. She sulks."

Nervous laugh with a chill in it.

I opened my eyes and said: "Thank God!" For

what I could see was a cerebral-gray ceiling, the shade you find only in the brain room of an advertising agency. I was safe in the arms of Fowler Schocken Associates—or was I? I didn't recognize the face that leaned over me.

"Why so pleased, Courtenay?" the face inquired. "Don't you know where you are?"

After that it was easy to guess. "Taunton's," I croaked.

"That is correct."

I tried my arms and legs and found they didn't respond. I couldn't tell whether it was drugs or a plasticocoon. "Look," I said steadily. "I don't know what you people think you're doing, but I advise you to stop it. Apparently this is a kidnaping for business purposes. You people are either going to let me go or kill me. If you kill me without a Notification you'll get the *cerebrin*, so of course you won't kill me. You're going to let me go eventually, so I suggest that you do it now."

"Kill you, Courtenay?" asked the face with mocking wonder. "How would we do that? You're dead already. Everybody knows that. You died on Starrzelius Glacier; don't you remember?"

I struggled again, without results. "They'll brainburn you," I said. "Are you people crazy? Who wants to be brainburned?"

The face said nonchalantly: "You'd be surprised." And in an aside to somebody else: "Tell Hedy he'll be ready soon." Hands did something, there was a click, and I was helped to sit up. The skin-tight pulling at my joints told me it was a plasticocoon and that I might save my strength. There was no point to struggling.

A buzzer buzzed and I was told sharply: "Keep

a respectful tongue in your head, Courtenay. Mr. Taunton's coming in."

B. J. Taunton lurched in, drunk. He looked just the way I had always seen him from afar at the speakers' table in hundreds of banquets: florid, gross, overdressed—and drunk.

He surveyed me, feet planted wide apart, hands on his hips, and swaying just a little. "Courtenay," he said. "Too bad. You might have turned out to be something if you hadn't cast your lot with that swindling son of a bitch Schocken. Too bad."

He was drunk, he was a disgrace to the profession, and he was responsible for crime after crime, but I couldn't keep my respect for an entrepreneur out of my voice. "Sir," I said evenly, "there must be some misunderstanding. There's been no provocation of Taunton Associates to commercial murder—has there?"

"Nope," he said, tight-lipped and swaying slightly. "Not as the law considers it provocation. All that bastard Schocken did was steal my groundwork, take over my Senators, suborn my committee witnesses, and *steal Venus from me!*" His voice had risen to an abrupt shriek. In a normal voice he continued: "No; no provocation. He's carefully refrained from killing any of my people. Shrewd Schocken; ethical Schocken; damned-fool Schocken!" he crooned.

His glassy eyes glared at me: "You bastard!" he said. "Of all the low-down, lousy, unethical, cheapjack stunts ever pulled on me, yours was the rottenest. *I*—" he thumped his chest, briefly threatening his balance. "*I* figured out a way to commit a safe commercial murder, and you played possum like a scared yellow rat. You ran like a rabbit, you dog."

"Sir," I said desperately, "I'm sure I don't know what you're driving at." His years of boozing, I thought briefly, had finally caught up with him. The words he was uttering could only come from a wet brain.

He sat down unconcernedly; one of his men darted in and there was a chair seat to meet his broad rump in the nick of time. With an expansive gesture B. J. Taunton said to me: "Courtenay, I am essentially an artist."

The words popped out of me automatically: "Of course, Mr.—" I almost said "Schocken." It was a well-conditioned reflex. "Of course, Mr. Taunton," I said.

"Essentially," he brooded, "essentially an artist. A dreamer of dreams; a weaver of visions." It gave me an uncanny sense of double vision. I seemed to see Fowler Schocken sitting there instead of his rival, the man who stood against everything that Fowler Schocken stood for. "I wanted Venus, Courtenay, and I shall have it. Schocken stole it from me, and I am going to repossess it. Fowler Schocken's management of the Venus project will stink to high heaven. No rocket under Schocken's management is ever going to get off the ground, if I have to corrupt every one of his underlings and kill every one of his section heads. For I am essentially an artist."

"Mr. Taunton," I said steadily, "you can't kill section heads as casually as all that. You'll be brain-burned. They'll give you *cerebrin*. You can't find anybody who'll take the risk for you. Nobody wants twenty years in hell."

He said dreamily: "I got a mechanic to drop that 'copter pod on you, didn't I? I got an unemployable bum to plug at you through your

135

apartment window, didn't I? Unfortunately both missed. And then you crossed us up with that cowardly run-out on the glacier."

I didn't say anything. The run-out on the glacier had been no idea of mine. God only knew whose idea it had been to have Runstead club me, shanghai me, and leave a substitute corpse in my place.

"Almost you escaped," Taunton mused. "If it hadn't been for a few humble, loyal servants—a taxi-runner, a few others—we never would have had you back. But I have my tools, Courtenay."

"They might be better, they might be worse, but it's my destiny to dream dreams and weave visions. The greatness of an artist is in his simplicity, Courtenay. You say to me: 'Nobody wants to be brainburned.' That is because you are mediocre. *I* say: '*Find* somebody who wants to be brainburned and *use* him.' That is because I am great."

"Wants to be brainburned," I repeated stupidly. "Wants to be brainburned."

"Explain," said Taunton to one aide. "I want him thoroughly convinced that we are in earnest."

One of his men told me dryly: "It's a matter of population, Courtenay. Have you ever heard of Albert Fish?"

"No."

"He was a phenomenon of the dawn; the earliest days of the Age of Reason—1920 or thereabouts. Albert Fish stuck needles into himself, burned himself with alcohol-saturated wads of cotton, flogged himself—he *liked* it. He would have liked brainburning, I'll wager. It would have been twenty delightful subjective years of being flayed, suffocated, choked, and nauseated. It would have been Albert Fish's dream come true.

136

"There was only one Albert Fish in his day. Pressures and strains of a very high order are required to produce an Albert Fish. It would be unreasonable to expect more than one to be produced out of the small and scattered population of the period—less than three billion. With our vastly larger current population there are many Albert Fishes wandering around. You only have to find them. Our matchless research facilities here at Taunton have unearthed several. They turn up at hospitals, sometimes in very grotesque shape. They are eager would-be killers; they want the delights of punishment. A man like you says we can't hire killers because they'd be afraid of being punished. But Mr. Taunton, now, says we *can* hire a killer if we find one who *likes* being punished. And the best part of it all is, the ones who like to get hurt are the ones who just love hurting others. Hurting, for instance—you."

It had a bloodcurdlingly truthful ring to it. Our generation must be inured to wonder. The chronicles of fantastic heroism and abysmal wickedness that crowd our newscasts—I knew from research that they didn't have such courage or such depravity in the old days. The fact had puzzled me. We have such people as Malone, who quietly dug his tunnels for six years and then one Sunday morning blew up Red Bank, New Jersey. A Brink's traffic cop had got him sore. Conversely we have James Revere, hero of the *White Cloud* disaster. A shy, frail tourist-class steward, he had rescued on his own shoulders seventy-six passengers, returning again and again into the flames with his flesh charring from his bones, blind, groping his way along red-hot bulkheads with his hand-stumps. It was true. When there are *enough* people, you will always find somebody who can and will be any given thing. Taunton *was* an artist. He had grasped this broad and simple truth and used it. It meant that I was as good as dead. *Kathy,* I thought. *My Kathy.*

Taunton's thick voice broke in on my reflections. "You grasp the pattern?" he asked. "The big picture? The theme, the message, what I might call the essential juice of it is that I'm going to repossess Venus. Now, beginning at the beginning, tell us about the Schocken Agency. All its little secrets, its little weaknesses, its ins and outs, its corruptible employees, its appropriations, its Washington contacts—*you* know."

I was a dead man with nothing to lose—I thought. "No," I said.

One of Taunton's men said abruptly: "He's ready for Hedy," got up and went out.

Taunton said: "You've studied prehistory, Courtenay. You may recognize the name of Gilles de Rais." I did, and felt a tightness over my scalp, like a steel helmet slowly shrinking. "All the generations of prehistory added up to an estimated five billion population," Taunton rambled. "All the generations of prehistory produced only one Gilles de Rais, whom you perhaps think of as Bluebeard. Nowadays we have our pick of several. Out of all the people I might have picked to handle special work like that for me I picked Hedy. You'll see why."

The door opened and a pale, adenoidal girl with lank blond hair was standing in it. She had a silly grin on her face; her lips were thin and bloodless. In one hand she held a six-inch needle set in a plastic handle.

I looked into her eyes and began screaming. I

couldn't stop screaming until they led her away and closed the door again. I was broken.

"Taunton," I whispered at last. "Please . . ."

He leaned back comfortably and said: "Give."

I tried, but I couldn't. My voice wouldn't work right and neither would my memory. I couldn't remember whether my firm was Fowler Schocken or Schocken Fowler, for instance.

Taunton got up at last and said: "We'll put you on ice for a while, Courtenay, so you can pull yourself together. I need a drink myself." He shuddered involuntarily, and then beamed again. "Sleep on it," he said, and left unsteadily.

Two of his men carted me from the brain room, down a corridor and into a bare cubbyhole with a very solid door. It seemed to be night in executives' country. Nothing was going on in any of the offices we passed, lights were low, and a single corridor guard was yawning at his desk.

I asked unsteadily: "Will you take the cocoon off me? I'm going to be a filthy mess if I don't get out of it."

"No orders about it," one of them said briefly, and they slammed the solid door and locked it. I flopped around the small floor trying to find something sharp enough to break the film and give me an even chance of bursting the plastic, but there was nothing. After incredible contortions and a dozen jarring falls I found that I could never get to my feet. The doorknob had offered a very, very faint ghost of hope, but it might as well have been a million miles away.

Mitchell Courtenay, copysmith. Mitchell Courtenay, key man of the Venus section. Mitchell Courtenay, destroyer-to-be of the Consies. Mitchell Courtenay flopping on the floor of a cell in the offices of the sleaziest, crookedest agency that ever blemished the profession, without any prospect except betrayal and—with luck—a merciful death. Kathy at least would never know. She would think I had died like a fool on the glacier, meddling with the power pack when I had no business to . . .

The lock of the door rattled and rattled. They were coming for me.

But when the door opened I saw from the floor not a forest of trousered legs but a single pair of matchstick ankles, nylon-clad.

"I love you," said the strange, dead voice of a woman. "They said I would have to wait, but I couldn't wait." It was Hedy. She had her needle.

I tried to cry for help, but my chest seemed paralyzed as she knelt beside me with shining eyes. The temperature of the room seemed to drop ten degrees. She clamped her bloodless lips on mine; they were like heated iron. And then I thought the left side of my face and head were being torn off. It lasted for seconds and blended into a red haze and unconsciousness.

"Wake up," the dead voice was saying. "I want you. Wake up." Lightning smashed at my right elbow, and I cried out and jerked my arm. My arm moved—

It moved.

The bloodless lips descended on mine again, and again her needle ran into my jaw, probing exactly for the great lump of the trigeminal facial nerve, and finding it. I fought the red haze that was trying to swallow me up. My arm had moved. She had perforated the membrane of the cocoon, and it could be burst. The needle searched again and somehow the pain was channeled to my right arm. In one convulsive jerk it was free.

I think I took the back of her neck in my hand and squeezed. I am not sure. I do not want to be sure. But after five minutes she and her love did not matter. I ripped and stripped the plastic from me and got to my feet an inch at a time, moaning from stiffness.

The corridor guard could not matter any more. If he had not come at my cries he would never come. I walked from the room and saw the guard apparently sleeping face-down on his desk. As I stood over him I saw a very little blood and serum puddled and coagulating in the small valley between the two cords of his shrunken old neck. One thrust transfixing the medulla had been enough for Hedy. I could testify that her knowledge of the nervous system's topography was complete.

The guard wore a gun that I hesitated over for a moment and then rejected. In his pockets were a few dollars that would be more useful. I hurried on to the ladders. His desk clock said 0605.

I knew already about climbing up stairs. I learned then about climbing down stairs. If your heart's in good shape there's little to choose between them. It took me an estimated thirty minutes in my condition to get down the ladders of executives' country and onto the populated stairs below. The first sullen stirrings of the workbound consumers were well under way. I passed half a dozen bitter fist fights and one cutting scrape. The Taunton Building nightdwellers were a low, dirty lot who never would have been allowed stairspace in the Schocken Tower, but it was all to the good. I attracted no attention what-

soever in my filthy clothes and sporting a fresh
stab wound in my face. Some of the bachelor girls
even whistled, but that was all. The kind of
people you have in the ancient, run-down slum
buildings like R.C.A. and Empire State would
have pulled me down if I'd taken their eye.

My timing was good. I left the building lobby
in the very core of a cheek-by-jowl mob boiling
out the door to the shuttle which would take them
to their wretched jobs. I thought I saw hardguys
in plain clothes searching the mob from second-
floor windows, but I didn't look up and I got into
the shuttle station.

At the change booth I broke all my bills and
went into the washroom. "Split a shower, bud?"
Somebody asked me. I wanted a shower terribly,
and by myself, but I didn't dare betray any white-
collar traits. She and I pooled our coins for a
five-minute salt, thirty-second fresh, with soap. I
found that I was scrubbing my right hand over
and over again. I found that when the cold water
hit the left side of my face the pain was dizzying.

After the shower I wedged myself into the shuttle and spent two hours zigzagging under the
city. My last stop was Times Square, in the heart
of the market district. It was mostly a freight station. While cursing consumers hurled crates of
protein ticketed for various parts of town onto
the belts I tried to phone Kathy again. Again there
was nobody home.

I got Hester at the Schocken Tower. I told her:
"I want you to raise every cent you can, borrow,
clean out your savings, buy a Starrzelius apparel
outfit for me, and meet me with it soonest at the
place where your mother broke her leg two years
ago. The exact place, remember?"

"Mitch," she said. "Yes, I remember. But my contract—"

"Don't make me beg you, Hester," I pleaded. "Trust me. I'll see you through. For God's sake, hurry. And—if you get here and I'm in the hands of the guards, don't recognize me. Now, into action."

I hung up and slumped in the phone booth until the next party hammered indignantly on the door. I walked slowly around the station, had Coffiest and a cheese sandwich, and rented a morning paper at the newsstand. The story about me was a bored little item on page three out of a possible four: SOUGHT FOR CB & FEMICIDE. It said George Groby had failed to return from pass to his job with Chlorella and had used his free time to burglarize executives' country in the Taunton Building. He had killed a secretary who stumbled on him and made his escape.

Hester met me half an hour later hard by the loading chute from which a crate had once whizzed to break her mother's leg. She looked frantically worried; technically she was as guilty of contract breach as "George Groby."

I took the garment box from her and asked: "Do you have fifteen hundred dollars left?"

"Just about. My mother was frantic—"

"Get us reservations on the next Moon ship; today if possible. Meet me back here; I'll be wearing the new clothes."

"Us? The Moon?" she squeaked.

"Yes; us. I've got to get off the Earth before I'm killed. And this time it'll be for keeps."

12

MY LITTLE HES-
ter squared her shoulders and proceeded to work
miracles.

In ten hours we were grunting side by side
under the take-off acceleration of the Moon ship
David Ricardo. She had cold-bloodedly passed
herself off as a Schocken employee on special detail to the Moon and me as Groby, a sales analyst
6. Naturally the dragnet for Groby, expediter
9, had not included the Astoria spaceport. Sewage
workers on the lam from CB and femicide
wouldn't have the money to hop a rocket, of
course.

We rated a compartment and the max ration.
The *David Ricardo* was so constructed that most
passengers rated compartments and max rations.
It wasn't a trip for the idly curious or the submerged fifteen sixteenths of the population. The
Moon was strictly business—mining business—and
some sight-seeing. Our fellow-passengers, what we
saw of them at the ramp, were preoccupied en-
gineers, a few laborers in the minute steerage,

and silly-rich men and women who wanted to say they'd been there.

After take-off, Hester was hysterically gay for a while, and then snapped. She sobbed on my shoulder, frightened at the enormity of what she'd done. She'd been brought up in a deeply moral, sales-fearing home, and you couldn't expect her to commit the high commercial crime of breaking a labor contract without there being a terrific emotional lashback.

She wailed: "Mr. Courtenay—Mitch—if only I could be *sure* it was all right! I know you've always been good to me and I know you wouldn't do anything wrong, but I'm so scared and miserable!"

I dried her eyes and made a decision.

"I'll tell you what it's all about, Hester," I said. "You be the judge. Taunton has discovered something very terrible. He's found out that there are people who are not deterred by the threat of *cerebrin* as the punishment for an unprovoked commercial murder. He thinks Mr. Schocken grabbed the Venus project from him unethically, and he'll stop at nothing to get it back. He's tried twice at least to kill me. I thought Mr. Runstead was one of his agents, assigned to bitch up Schocken's handling of the Venus account. Now, I don't know. Mr. Runstead clubbed me when I went after him at the South Pole, spirited me away to a labor freighter under a faked identity, and left a substitute body for mine. And," I said cautiously, "there are Consies in it."

She uttered a small shriek.

"I don't know how they dovetail," I said. "But I was in a Consie cell—"

"Mis-ter *Courtenay!*"

"Strictly as a blind," I hastily explained. "I was stuck in Chlorella Costa Rica and the only way north seemed to be through the Consie network. They had a cell in the factory, I joined up, turned on the talent, and got transferred to New York. The rest you know."

She paused for a long time and asked: "Are you sure it's all right?"

Wishing desperately that it were, I firmly said: "Of course, Hester."

She gave me a game smile. "I'll get our rations," she said, unsnapping herself. "You'd better stay here."

Forty hours out I said to Hester: "The blasted blackmarketing steward is going too far! Look at this!" I held up my bulb of water and my ration box. The seal had clearly been tampered with on both containers, and visibly there was water missing. "Max rations," I went on oratorically, "are supposed to be tamper-proof, but this is plain burglary. How do yours look?"

"Same thing," she said listlessly. "You can't do anything about it. Let's not eat just yet, Mr. Courtenay." She made a marked effort to be vivacious. "Tennis, anyone?"

"All right," I grumbled, and set up the field, borrowed from the ship recreation closet. She was better at tennis than I, but I took her in straight sets. Her co-ordination was 'way off. She'd stab for a right forecourt deep cross-court return and like as not miss the button entirely—if she didn't send the ball into the net by failing to surge power with her left hand on the rheostat. A half hour of the exercise seemed to do both of us good. She cheered up and ate her rations and I had mine.

The tennis match before meals became a tradition. There was little enough to do in our cramped quarters. Every eight hours she would go for our tagged rations, I would grumble about the shortage and tampering, we'd have some tennis, and then eat. The rest of the time passed somehow, watching the ads come and go—all Schocken—on the walls. Well enough, I thought. Schocken's on the Moon and I won't be kept from him there. Things weren't so crowded. Moon to Schocken to Kathy—a twinge of feeling. I could have asked casually what Hester had heard about Jack O'Shea, but I didn't. I was afraid I might not like what she might have heard about the midget hero and his triumphal procession from city to city and woman to woman.

A drab service announcement at last interrupted the parade of ads: COOKS TO THE GALLEY (the *David Ricardo* was a British ship) FOR FINAL LIQUID FEEDING. THIS IS H-8 AND NO FURTHER SOLID OR LIQUID FOOD SHOULD BE CONSUMED UNTIL TOUCHDOWN.

Hester smiled and went out with our tray.

As usual it was ten minutes before she returned. We were getting some pull from the Moon by then: enough to unsettle my stomach. I burped miserably while waiting.

She came back with two Coffiest bulbs and reproached me gaily: "Why, Mitch, you haven't set up the tennis court!"

"Didn't feel like it. Let's eat." I put out my hand for my bulb. She didn't give it to me. "Well?"

"Just one set?" she coaxed.

"Hell, girl, you heard me," I snapped. "Let's not forget who's who around here." I wouldn't have said it if it hadn't been Coffiest, I suppose. The Starrzelius-red bulb kicked things off in me —nagging ghosts of withdrawal symptoms. I'd been off the stuff for a long time, but you never kick Coffiest.

She stiffened. "I'm sorry, Mr. Courtenay." And then she clutched violently at her middle, her face distorted. Astounded, I grabbed her. She was deathly pale and limp; she moaned with pain.

"Hester," I said, "what is it? What—?"

"Don't drink it," she croaked, her hand kneading her belly. "The Coffiest. Poison. Your rations. I've been tasting them." Her nails tore first the nylon of her midriff and then her skin as she clawed at the pain.

"Send a doctor!" I was yelling into the compartment mike. "Woman's dying here!"

The chief steward's voice answered me: "Right away, sir. Ship's doctor'll be there right away."

Hester's contorted face began to relax, frightening me terribly. She said softly: "Bitch Kathy. Running out on you. Mitch and bitch. Funny. You're too good for her. *She* wouldn't have. My life. Yours." There was another spasm across her face. "Wife versus secretary. A laugh. It always was. You never even kissed me—"

I didn't get a chance to. She was gone, and the ship's doctor was hauling himself briskly in along the handline. His face fell. We towed her to the lazarette and he put her in a cardiac-node exciter that started her heart going again. Her chest began to rise and fall and she opened her eyes.

"Where—are—you?" asked the doctor, loudly and clearly. She moved her head slightly, and a pulse of hope shot through me.

"Response?" I whispered to the doctor.

"Random," he said with professional coldness. He was right. There were more slight head movements and a nervous flutter of the eyelids, which were working independently. He kept trying with questions. "Who—are—you?" brought a wrinkle between her eyes, and a tremor of the lip, but no more. Except for a minute, ambiguous residue, she was gone.

Gently enough, the doctor began to explain to me: "I'm going to turn it off. You mustn't think there's any hope left. Evidently irreversible clinical death has occurred. It's often hard for a person with emotional ties to believe—"

I watched her eyelids flutter, one with a two-four beat, the other with a three-four beat. "Turn it off," I said hoarsely. By "it" I meant Hester and not the machine. He cut the current and withdrew the needle.

"There was nausea?" he asked. I nodded. "Her first space flight?" I nodded. "Abdominal pain?" I nodded. "No previous distress?" I shook my head. "History of vertigo?" I nodded, though I didn't know. He was driving at something. He kept asking, and the answers he wanted were as obvious as a magician's forced card. Allergies, easy bleeding, headaches, painful menses, afternoon fatigue—at last he said decisively: "I believe it's Fleischman's Disease. We don't know much about it. It stems from some derangement of function in the adrenocorticotropic bodies under free flight, we think. It kicks off a chain reaction of tissue-incompatibilities which affects the cerebrospinal fluid—"

He looked at me and his tone changed. "I have some alcohol in the locker," he said. "Would you like—"

149

I reached for the bulb and then remembered. "Have one with me," I said.

He nodded and, with no stalling, drank from one of the nipples of a twin-valve social flask. I saw his Adam's apple work. "Not too much," he cautioned me. "Touchdown's soon."

I stalled with conversation for a few minutes, watching him, and then swallowed half a pint of hundred proof. I could hardly tow myself back to the compartment.

Hangover, grief, fear, and the maddening red tape of Moon debarkation. I must have acted pretty stupidly. A couple of times I heard crewmen say to port officials something like: "Take it easy on the guy. He lost his girl in flight."

The line I took in the cramped receiving room of the endless questionnaires was that I didn't know anything about the mission. I was Groby, a 6, and the best thing to do would be to send me to Fowler Schocken. I understood that we had been supposed to report to him. They pooh-poohed that possibility and set me to wait on a bench while queries were sent to the Schocken branch in Luna City.

I waited and watched and tried to think. It wasn't easy. The busy crowds in Receiving were made up of people going from one place to another place to do specified things. I didn't fit in the pattern; I was a sore thumb. They were going to get me . . .

A tube popped and blinked at the desk yards away. I read between half-closed eyes: S-C-H-O-C-K-E-N T-O R-E-C-E-I-V-I-N-G R-E Q-U-E-R-Y N-O M-I-S-S-I-O-N D-U-E T-H-I-S F-L-I-G-H-T N-O G-R-O-B-Y E-M-P-L-O-Y-E-D B-Y U-S

F-O-W-L-E-R S-C-H-O-C-K-E-N U-N-Q-U-E-R-I-E-D B-U-T I-M-P-O-S-S-I-B-L-E- A-N-Y U-N-D-E-R S-T-A-R-C-L-A-S-S P-E-R-S-O-N-N-E-L A-S-S-I-G-N-E-D R-E-P-O-R-T H-I-M A-C-T D-I-S-C-R-E-T-I-O-N O-B-V-I-O-U-S-L-Y N-O-T O-U-R B-A-B-Y E-N-D

End indeed. They were glancing at me from the desk, and talking in low tones. In only a moment they would be beckoning the Burns Detective guards standing here and there.

I got up from the bench and sauntered into the crowd, with only one alternative left and that a frightening one. I made the casual gesture that, by their order and timing, constitute the Grand Hailing Sign of Distress of the Consies.

A Burns guard shouldered his way through the crowd and put the arm on me. "Are you going to make trouble?" he demanded.

"No," I said thickly. "Lead the way."

He waved confidently at the desk and they waved back, with grins. He marched me, with his nightstick in the small of my back, through the startled crowd. Numbly I let him take me from the receiving dome down a tunnel-like shopping street.

SOUVENIRS OF LUNA
CHEAPEST IN TOWN

YE TAYSTEE GOODIE SHOPPE ON YE MOONE

YOUR HOMETOWN PAPER

MOONSUITS RENTED
"50 Years Without a Blowout"

RELIABLE MOONSUIT RENTAL CO.
"73 Years Without a Blowout"

MOONMAID FASHIONS
Stunning Conversation Pieces
Prove You Were Here

Warren Astron, D.P.S.
Readings by Appointment Only

blinked and twinkled at me from the shopfronts as new arrivals sauntered up and down, gaping.

"Hold it," growled the guard. We stopped in front of the *Warren Astron* sign. He muttered: "Twist the nightstick away from me. Hit me a good lick over the head with it. Fire one charge at the streetlight. Duck into Astron's and give him the grip. Good luck—and try not to break my skull."

"You're—you're—" I stammered.

"Yeah," he said wryly. "I wish I hadn't seen the hailing sign. This is going to cost me two stripes and a raise. Get moving."

I did. He surrendered the nightstick, and I tried not to make it too easy or too hard when I clouted him. The buckshot charge boomed out of the stick's muzzle, shattered the light overhead, and brought forth shrieks of dismay from the strollers. It was thunderous in the vaulted street. I darted through the chaste white Adam door of Astron's in the sudden darkness and blinked at a tall, thin man with a goatee.

"What's the meaning of this?" he demanded. "I read by appointment—" I took his arm in the grip. "Refuge?" he asked, abruptly shedding a fussy professional manner.

"Yes. Fast."

He led me through his parlor into a small, high observatory with a transparent dome, a refracting telescope, Hindu star maps, clocks and desks. One of these desks he heaved on mightily, and it turned back on hinges. There was a pit and handholds. "Down you go," he said.

Down I went, into darkness.

It was some six feet deep and six by four in area. It had a rough, unfinished feel to it. There was a pick and shovel leaned against one wall, and a couple of buckets filled with moonrock. Obviously a work in progress.

I inverted one of the buckets and sat on it in the dark. After five hundred and seventy-six counted pulse-beats I sat on the floor and stopped counting. After that got too rugged I tried to brush moonrock out of the way and lie down. After going through this cycle five times I heard voices directly overhead. One was the fussy, professional voice of Astron. The other was the globby, petulant voice of a fat woman. They seemed to be seated at the desk which sealed my hidey-hole.

"—really seems excessive, my dear doctor."

"As Madam wishes. If you will excuse me, I shall return to my ephemeris—"

"But Dr. Astron, I wasn't implying—"

"Madam will forgive me for jumping to the conclusion that she was unwilling to grant me my customary honorarium . . . that is correct. Now, please, the birth date and hour?"

She mumbled them, and I wondered briefly about the problem Astron must have with women who shaded their years.

"So . . . Venus in the house of Mars . . . Mercury ascendant in the trine . . ."

"What's that?" she asked with shrill suspicion. "I know quite a bit about the Great Art and I never heard that before."

Blandly: "Madam must realize that a Moon observatory makes possible many things of which she has never heard before. It is possible by lunar observation to refine the Great Art to a point unattainable in the days when observations were made perforce through the thick and muddled air of Earth."

"Oh—oh, of course. I've heard that, of course. Please go on, Dr. Astron. Will I be able to look through your telescope and see my planets?"

"Later, madam. So . . . Mercury ascendant in the trine, the planet of strife and chicanery, yet quartered with Jupiter, the giver of fortune, so . . ."

The "reading" lasted perhaps half an hour, and there were two more like it that followed, and then there was silence. I actually dozed off until a voice called me. The desk had been heaved back again and Astron's head was silhouetted against the rectangular opening. "Come on out," he said. "It's safe for twelve hours."

I climbed out stiffly and noted that the observatory dome had been opaqued.

"You're Groby," he stated.

"Yes," I said, dead-pan.

"We got a report on you by courier aboard the *Ricardo*. God knows what you're up to; it's too much for me." I noticed that his hand was in his pocket. "You turn up in Chlorella, you're a natural-born copysmith, you're transferred to New York, you get kidnaped in front of the Met—in earnest or by prearrangement—you kill a girl and disappear—and now you're on the Moon. God knows what you're up to. It's too much for me. A Central Committee member will be here shortly to try and figure you out. Is there anything you'd care to say? Like confessing that you're an *agent provocateur?* Or subject to manic-depressive psychosis?"

I said nothing.

"Very well," he said. Somewhere a door opened and closed. "That will be she," he told me.

And my wife Kathy walked into the observatory.

13

"MITCH," SHE said dazedly. "My God, Mitch." She laughed, with a note of hysteria. "You wouldn't wait, would you? You wouldn't stay on ice."

The astrologer took the gun out of his pocket and asked her: "Is there—?"

"No, Warren. It's all right. I know him. You can leave us alone. Please."

He left us alone. Kathy dropped into a chair, trembling. I couldn't move. My wife was a kingpin Consie. I had thought I'd known her, and

I'd been wrong. She had lied to me continuously and I had never known it.

"Aren't you going to say anything?" I asked flatly.

She visibly took hold of herself. "Shocked?" she asked. "You, a star-class copysmith consorting with a Consie? Afraid it'll get out and do you no good businesswise?" She forced a mocking smile that broke down as I looked at her. "Damn it," she flared, "all I ever asked from you after I came to my senses was for you to get out of my life and stay out. The biggest mistake I ever made was keeping Taunton from killing you."

"You had Runstead shanghai me?"

"Like a fool. What in God's name are you doing here? What are these wild-man stunts of yours? Why can't you leave me alone?" She was screaming by then.

Kathy a Consie. Runstead a Consie. Deciding what was best for poor Mitch and doing it. Taunton deciding what was best for poor Mitch and doing it. Moving me this way and that across the chessboard.

"Pawn queens," I said, and picked her up and slapped her. The staring intensity left her eyes and she looked merely surprised. "Get what's-his-name in here," I said.

"Mitch, what are you up to?" She sounded like herself.

"Get him in here."

"You can't order me—"

"You!" I yelled. "The witch-doctor!"

He came running, right into my fist. Kathy was on my back, a clawing wildcat, as I went through his pockets. I found the gun—a wicked .25 UHV machine pistol—and shoved her to the floor. She

156

looked up at me in astonishment, mechanically rubbing a bruised hip. "You're a mean son of a bitch," she said wonderingly.

"All of a sudden," I agreed. "Does Fowler Schocken know you're on the Moon?"

"No," she said, rubbing her thumb and forefinger together.

"You're lying."

"My little lie-detector," she crooned jeeringly. "My little fire-eating copysmith—"

"Level with me," I said, "or you get this thing across the face."

"Good God," she said. "You mean it." She put her hand to her face slowly, looking at the gun.

"I'm glad that's settled. Does Fowler Schocken know you're on the Moon?"

"Not exactly," she said, still watching the gun. "He did advise me to make the trip—to help me get over my bereavement."

"Call him. Get him here."

She didn't say anything or move to the phone.

"Listen," I said. "This is Groby talking. Groby's been slugged, knifed, robbed, and kidnaped. He saw the only friend he had in the world poisoned a few hours ago. He's been played with by a lady sadist who knew her anatomy lessons. He killed her for it and he was glad of it. He's so deep in hock to Chlorella that he'll never get out. He's wanted for femicide and CB. The woman he thought he was in love with turned out to be a lying fanatic and a bitch. Groby has nothing to lose. I can put a burst through the dome up there and we'll all suck space. I can walk out into the street, give myself up, and tell exactly what I know. They won't believe me but they'll investigate to make sure, and sooner or later they'll get corroboration—after I've been brainburned, but that doesn't matter. I've nothing to lose."

"And," she asked flatly, "what have you got to gain?"

"Stop stalling. Call Schocken."

"Not without one more try, Mitch. One word hurt specially—'fanatic.' There were two reasons why I begged Runstead to shanghai you. I wanted you out of the way of Taunton's killers. And I wanted you to get a taste of the consumer's life. I thought—I don't know. I thought you'd see how fouled-up things have become. It's hard to see when you're star class. From the bottom it's easier to see. I thought I'd be able to talk sense to you after we brought you back to life, and we'd be able to work together on the only job worth doing. So it didn't work. That damned brain of yours —so good and so warped. All you want is to be star class again and eat and drink and sleep a little better than anybody else. It's too bad you're not a fanatic too. Same old Mitch. Well, I tried.

"Go ahead and do whatever you think you have to do. Don't fret about it hurting me. It's not going to hurt worse than the nights we used to spend screaming at each other. Or the times I was out on Consie business and couldn't tell you and had to watch you being jealous. Or shipping you to Chlorella to try and make you a whole sane man in spite of what copysmithing's done to you. Or never being able to love you all the way, never being able to give myself to you entirely, mind or body, because there was this secret. I've been hurt. Pistol-whipping's a joke compared to the way I've been hurt."

There was a pause that seemed to go on forever.

158

"Call Schocken," I said unsteadily. "Tell him to come here. Then get out and take the stargazer with you. I—I don't know what I'm going to tell him. But I'm going to give you and your friends a couple of days' grace. Time to change headquarters and hailing signs and the rest of your insane rigmarole. Call Schocken and get out of here. I don't ever want to see you again."

I couldn't read the look on her face as she picked up the phone and punched a number.

"Mr. Schocken's sec³, please," she said. "This is Dr. Nevin—widow of Mr. Courtenay. You'll find me on the through list, I believe . . . thank you. Mr. Schocken's sec², please. This is Dr. Nevin, Mr. Courtenay's widow. May I speak to Mr. Schocken's secretary? I'm listed . . . thank you . . . Hello, Miss Grice; this is Dr. Nevin. May I speak to Mr. Schocken? . . . Certainly . . . thank you . . ." She turned to me and said: "I'll have to wait a few moments." They passed in silence, and then she said: "Hello, Mr. Schocken . . . Well, thank you. I wonder if you could come and see me about a matter of importance . . . business *and* personal . . . the sooner the better, I'm afraid . . . Shopping One, off Receiving—Dr. Astron's . . . no, nothing like that. It's just a convenient meeting place. Thank you very much, Mr. Schocken."

I wrenched the phone from her and heard Fowler Schocken's voice say: "Quite all right, my dear. The mystery is intriguing. Good-by." *Click.* She was quite clever enough to have faked a one-sided conversation, but had not. The voice was unmistakable. The memories it brought back of Board mornings with their brilliance of dialectic interplay, hard and satisfying hours of work climaxed with a "Well done!" and shrewd guidance through the intricacies of the calling overwhelmed me with nostalgia. I was almost home.

Silently and efficiently Kathy was shouldering the stargazer's limp body. Without a word she walked from the observatory. A door opened and closed.

The hell with her . . .

It was minutes before there was a jovial halloo in the voice of Fowler Schocken: "Kathy! Anybody home?"

"In here," I called.

Two of our Brink's men and Fowler Schocken came in. His face went mottled purple. "Where's —" he began. And then: "You look like—*you are! Mitch!*" he grabbed me and waltzed me hilariously around the circular room while the guards dropped their jaws. "What kind of a trick was that to play on an old man? What's the story, boy? Where's Kathy?" He stopped, puffing even under moonweight.

"I've been doing some undercover work," I said. "I'm afraid I've got myself into some trouble. Would you call for more guards? We may have to stand off Luna City Inc.'s Burns men." Our Brink's men, who took an artisan's pride in their work, grinned happily at the thought.

"Sure, Mitch. Get it done," he said sidewise to the sergeant, who went happily to the phone. "Now what's all this about?"

"For the present," I said, "let's say it's been a field trip that went sour. Let's say I downgraded myself temporarily and voluntarily to assess Venus Section sentiment among the consumers—and I got stuck. Fowler, please let me beg off any more

160

details. I'm in a bad way. Hungry, tired, scared, dirty."

"All right, Mitch. You know my policy. Find a good horse, give him his head, and back him to the limit. You've never let me down—and God knows I'm glad to see you around again. Venus Section can use you. Nothing's going right. The indices are down to 3.77 composite for North America when they should be 4.0 and rising. And turnover? God! I'm here recruiting, you know: a little raid on Luna City Inc., Moonmines, and the other outfits for some space-seasoned executives."

It was good to be home. "Who's heading it up?" I asked.

"I am. We rotated a few Board men through the spot and there wasn't any pickup. In spite of my other jobs I had to take over Venus Section direct. *Am* I glad to see you!"

"Runstead?"

"He's vice-ing for me, poor man. What's this jam you're in with the guards? Where's Kathy?"

"Please, later . . . I'm wanted for femicide and CB on Earth. Here I'm a suspicious character without clearance. Also I resisted arrest, clouted a guard, and damaged Luna City property."

He looked grave. "You know, I don't like the sound of CB," he said. "I assume there was a flaw in the contract?"

"Several," I assured him.

He brightened. "Then we'll pay off the fines on the rest of the stuff and fight the CB clear up to the Chamber of Commerce if we have to. What firm?"

"Chlorella Costa Rica."

"Hmmm. Middling-sized, but solid. Excellent

people, all of them. A pleasure to do business with."

Not from the bottom up, I thought, and said nothing.

"I'm sure they'll be reasonable. And if they aren't, I have a majority of the C of C in my pocket anyway. I ought to get something for my retainers, eh?" He dug me slyly in the ribs. His relief at getting Venus Section off his neck was overwhelming.

A dozen of our Brink's boys churned in. "That should do it," Fowler Schocken beamed. "Lieutenant, the Luna City Inc. Burns people may try to take Mr. Courtenay here away from us. We don't want that to happen, do we?"

"No, sir," said the lieutenant, dead-pan.

"Then let's go."

We strolled down Shopping One, amazing a few night-owl tourists. Shopping One gave way to Residential One, Two, and Three, and then to Commercial One.

"Hey, you!" a stray Burns patrolman called. We were in somewhat open order. Evidently he didn't realize that the Brink's men were my escort.

"Go play with your marbles, Punchy," a sergeant told him.

He went pale, but beeped his alarm, and went down in a tangle of fists and boots.

Burns patrolmen came bounding along the tunnel-like street in grotesque strides. Faces appeared in doorways. Our detail's weapons-squad leader said: *"Hup!"* and his boys began to produce barrels, legs, belts of ammo, and actions from their uniforms. Snap-snap-snap-snap, and there were two machine guns mounted on the right tripod ready to rake both ends of the street. The Burns men braked grotesquely yards from us and stood unhappily, swinging their nightsticks.

Our lieutenant called out: "What seems to be the trouble, gentlemen?"

A Burns man called back: "Is that man George Groby?"

"Are you George Groby?" the lieutenant asked me.

"No. I'm Mitchell Courtenay."

"You hear him," the lieutenant called. The weapons men full-cocked their guns at a signal from the squad leader. The two clicks echoed from the vaulting, and the few last-ditch rubbernecks hanging from the doors vanished.

"Oh," said the Burns man weakly. "That's all right then. You can go ahead." He turned on the rest of the patrolmen. "Well? What are you dummies waiting for? Didn't you hear me?" They beat it, and we moved on down Commercial One, with the weapons men cradling their guns. The Fowler Schocken Associates Luna City Branch was 75 Commercial One, and we went in whistling. The weapons men mounted their guns in the lobby.

It was a fantastic performance. I had never seen its like. Fowler Schocken explained it as he led me down into the heart of the agency. "It's frontier stuff, Mitch. Something you've got to get into your copy. 'The Equalizer' is what they call it. A man's rank doesn't mean much up here. A well-drilled weapons squad is the law topside of the stratosphere. It's getting back to the elemental things of life, where a man's a man no matter how high his Social Security number."

We passed a door. "O'Shea's room," he said. "He isn't in yet, of course. The little man's out gathering rosebuds while he may—and the time isn't going to be long. The only Venus roundtripper. We'll lick that, won't we, Mitch?"

He showed me into a cubicle and lowered the bed with his own hands. "Cork off with these," he said, producing a sheaf of notes from his breast pocket. "Just some rough jottings for you to go over. I'll send in something to eat and then Coffiest. A good hour or two of work on them, and then the sound sleep of the just, eh?"

"Yes, Mr. Schocken."

He beamed at me and left, drawing the curtain. I stared glazedly at the rough jottings. "Six-color doubletrux. Downhold unsuccessful previous flights. Cite Learoyd 1959, Holden 1961, McGill 2002 et al heroic pioneers supreme sacrifice etc etc. *No* mention Myers-White flopperoo 2010 acct visibly exploded bfr passng moon orbit. Try get M-W taken out of newssheet files & history bks? Get cost estimate. Search archives for pix LH & McG. Shd be blond brunet & redhead. Ships in backgrnd. Looming. Panting woman but heroic pioneers dedicated look in eye not interested. Piquant bcs unavlbl . . ."

Thoughtfully, there was a pencil and copy-paper in the cubicle. I began to write painfully: "We were ordinary guys. We liked the earth and the good things it gave us. The morning tang of Coffiest . . . the first drag on a Starr . . . the good feel of a sharp new Verily pinstripe suit . . . a warm smile from a girl in a bright spring dress—but they weren't enough. There were far places we had to see, things we had to know. The little guy's Learoyd. Nineteen fifty-nine. I'm Holden. Nineteen sixty-one. The redhead with the shoulders is McGill—twenty oh-two. Yes; we're dead. But we saw the far places and we learned what we had to learn before we died. Don't pity us; we did it for you. The long-hair astronomers could only guess about Venus. Poison gas, they said. Winds so hot they'd set your hair on fire and so strong they'd pick you up and throw you away. But they weren't sure. What do you do when you aren't sure? You go and see."

A guard came in with sandwiches and Coffiest. I munched and gulped with one hand and wrote with the other.

"We had good ships for those days. They packed us and enough fuel to get us there. What they didn't have was enough fuel to get us back. But don't pity us; we had to know. There was always the chance that the long-hairs were wrong, that we'd be able to get out, breathe clean air, swim in cool water—and then make fuel for the return trip with the good news. No; it didn't work out that way. It worked out that the long-hairs knew their stuff. Learoyd didn't wait to starve in his crate; he opened the hatch and breathed methane after writing up his log. My crate was lighter. The wind picked it up and broke it—and me with it. McGill had extra rations and a heavier ship. He sat and wrote for a week and then—well; it was pretty certain after two no-returns. He'd taken cyanide with him. But don't pity us. We went there and we saw it and in a way we sent back the news by not coming back ourselves. Now you folks know what to do and how to do it. You know the long-hairs weren't guessing. Venus is a mean lady and you've got to take the stuff and the know-how to tame her. She'll treat you right when you do. When you find us and our crates don't pity us. We did it for you. We knew you wouldn't let us down."

I was home again.

14

"PLEASE, FOWLER," I said. "Tomorrow. Not today."

He gave me a steady look. "I'll go along, Mitch," he said. "I've never been a back-seat driver yet." He displayed one of the abilities that made him boss-man. He wiped clean out of his mind the burning curiosity about where I had been and what I had been doing. "That's good copy," he said, slapping my work of the previous night on his desk. "Clear it with O'Shea, won't you? He can give it some extra see-taste-smell-hear-feel if anybody can. And pack for return aboard the *Vilfredo Pareto*—I forgot. You haven't got anything to pack. Here's some scratch, and shop when you get a chance. Take a few of the boys with you, of course. The Equalizer—remember?" He twinkled at me.

I went to find O'Shea curled up like a cat in

the middle of his full-sized bunk in the cubicle next to mine. The little man looked ravaged when he rolled over and stared blearily at me. "Mitch," he said thickly. " 'Nother goddam nightmare."

"Jack," I said persuasively. "Wake up, Jack."

He jerked bolt upright and glared at me. "What's the idea—? Hello, Mitch. I remember. Somebody said something when I got in 'smorning." He held his small head. "I'm dying," he said faintly. "Get me something, will you? My death-bed advice is this: don't ever be a hero. You're too nice a guy . . ."

The midget lapsed into torpor, swaying a little with each pulsebeat. I went to the kitchen and punched Coffiest, Thiamax, and a slice of Bredd. Halfway out, I returned, went to the bar, and punched two ounces of bourbon.

O'Shea looked at the tray and hiccuped. "What the hell's that stuff?" he said faintly, referring to the Coffiest, Thiamax, and Bredd. He shot down the bourbon and shuddered.

"Long time no see, Jack," I said.

"Ooh," he groaned. "Just what I needed. Why do clichés add that extra something to a hang-over?" He tried to stand up to his full height of thirty-five inches and collapsed back onto the cot, his legs dangling. "My aching back," he said. "I think I'm going to enter a monastery. I'm living up to my reputation, and it's killing me by inches. Ooh, that tourist gal from Nova Scotia! It's spring-time, isn't it? Do you think that explains anything? Maybe she has Eskimo blood."

"It's late fall," I said.

"Urp. Maybe she doesn't have a calendar . . . pass me that Coffiest." No "Please." And no "thank you." Just a cool, take-it-for-granted that the world was his for the asking. He had changed.

"Think you can do some work this morning?" I asked, a little stiffly.

"I might," he said indifferently. "This is Schocken's party after all. Say, what the hell ever became of you?"

"I've been investigating," I said.

"Seen Kathy?" he asked. "That's a wonderful girl you have there, Mitch." His smile might have been reminiscent. All I was sure of was that I didn't like it—not at all.

"Glad you enjoyed her," I said flatly. "Drop in any time." He sputtered into his Coffiest and said, carefully setting it down: "What's that work you mentioned?"

I showed him my copy. He gulped the Thiamax and began to steady on his course as he read.

"You got it all fouled up," he said at last, scornfully. "I don't know Learoyd, Holden, and McGill from so many holes in the ground, but like hell they were selfless explorers. You don't get *pulled* to Venus. You get *pushed*." He sat brooding, cross-legged.

"We're assuming they got pulled," I said. "If you like, we're trying to convince people that they got pulled. What we want from you is sense-impressions to sprinkle the copy with. Just talking off the front of your face, how do you resonate to it?"

"With nausea," he said, bored. "Would you reserve me a shower, Mitch? Ten minutes fresh, 100 degrees. Damn the cost. You too can be a celebrity. All you have to do is be lucky like me." He swung his short legs over the edge of the cot and contemplated his toes, six inches clear of the floor. "Well," he sighed, "I'm getting it while the getting's good."

"What about my copy?" I asked.

"See my reports," he said. "What about my shower?"

"See your valet," I said, and went out, boiling. In my own cubicle I sweated sense-impressions into the copy for a couple of hours and then picked up a guard squad to go shopping. There were no brushes with the patrolmen. I noticed that Warren Astron's shopfront now sported a chaste sign:

> *Dr. Astron Regrets That*
> *Urgent Business*
> *Has Recalled Him to Earth on*
> *Short Notice*

I asked one of our boys: "Has the *Ricardo* left?"

"Couple hours ago, Mr. Courtenay. Next departure's the *Pareto*, tomorrow."

So I could talk.

So I told Fowler Schocken the whole story.

And Fowler Schocken didn't believe a Goddamned word of it.

He was nice enough and he tried not to hurt my feelings. "Nobody's blaming you, Mitch," he said kindly. "You've been through a great strain. It happens to us all, this struggle with reality. Don't feel you're alone, my boy. We'll see this thing through. There are times when anybody needs—help. My analyst—"

I'm afraid I yelled at him.

"Now, now," he said, still kind and understanding. "Just to pass the time—laymen shouldn't dabble in these things, but I think I know a thing or two about it and can discuss it objectively—let me try to explain—"

"Explain *this!*" I shouted at him, thrusting my altered Social Security tattoo under his nose.

"If you wish," he said calmly. "It's part of the whole pattern of your brief—call it a holiday from reality. You've been on a psychological bender. You got away from yourself. You assumed a new identity, and you chose one as far-removed from your normal, hard-working, immensely able self as possible. You chose the lazy, easy-going life of a scum-skimmer, drowsing in the tropic sun—"

I knew then who was out of touch with reality.

"Your horrible slanders against Taunton are crystal-clear to, ah, a person with some grasp of our unconscious drives. I was pleased to hear you voice them. They meant that you're halfway back to your real self. What is our central problem—the central problem of the real Mitchell Courtenay, copysmith? Lick the opposition! Crush the competing firms! Destroy them! Your fantasy about Taunton indicates to, ah, an informed person that you're struggling back to the real Mitchell Courtenay, copysmith. Veiled in symbols, obscured by ambivalent attitudes, the Taunton-fantasy is nevertheless clear. Your imagined encounter with the girl 'Hedy' might be a textbook example!"

"God damn it," I yelled, "look at my jaw! See that hole? It still hurts!"

He just smiled and said: "Let's be glad you did nothing worse to yourself, Mitch. The id, you see—"

"What about Kathy?" I asked hoarsely. "What about the complete data on the Consies I gave you? Grips, hailing signs, passwords, meeting places?"

"Mitch," he said earnestly, "as I say, I shouldn't be meddling, but they aren't real. Sexual hostility unleashed by the dissociation of your personality into 'Groby'-Courtenay identified your wife with a hate-and-fear object, the Consies. And 'Groby' carefully arranged things so that your Consie data is uncheckable and therefore unassailable. 'Groby' arranged for you—the *real* you—to withhold the imaginary 'data' until the Consies would have had a chance to change all that. 'Groby' was acting in self-defense. Courtenay was coming back and he knew it; 'Groby' felt himself being 'squeezed out.' Very well; he can bide his time. He arranged things so that he can make a comeback—"

"I'm not insane!"

"My analyst—!"

"You've got to believe me!"

"These unconscious conflicts—"

"I tell you Taunton has killers!"

"Do you know what convinced me, Mitch?"

"What?" I asked bitterly.

"The fantasy of a Consie cell embedded in Chicken Little. The symbolism—" he flushed a little, "well, it's quite unmistakable."

I gave up except on one point: "Do people still humor the insane, Mr. Schocken?"

"You're *not* insane, my boy. You need—help, like a lot of—"

"I'll be specific. Will you humor me in one respect?"

"Of course," he grinned, humoring me.

"Guard yourself and me too. Taunton has killers—all right; I think, or Groby thinks, or some damn body thinks that Taunton has killers. If you humor me to the extent of guarding yourself and me, I promise not to start swinging from the ceiling and gibbering. I'll even go to your analyst."

"All right," he smiled, humoring me.

Poor old Fowler. Who could blame him? His own dream-world was under attack by every word I had to say. My story was blasphemy against the god of Sales. He couldn't believe it, and he couldn't believe that I—the real I—believed it. How could Mitchell Courtenay, copysmith, be sitting there and telling him such frightful things as:

> The interests of producers and consumers are not identical;

> Most of the world is unhappy;

> Workmen don't automatically find the job they do best;

> Entrepreneurs don't play a hard, fair game by the rules;

> The Consies are sane, intelligent, and well organized.

They were hammer-blows at him, but Fowler Schocken was nothing if not resilient. The hammer bounced right off and the dents it made were ephemeral. There was an explanation for everything and Sales could do no wrong. Therefore, Mitchell Courtenay, copysmith, was not sitting there telling him these things. It was Mitchell Courtenay's wicked, untamed id or the diabolic 'George Groby' or somebody—anybody but Courtenay.

In a dissociated fashion that would have delighted Fowler Schocken and his analyst I said to myself: "You know, Mitch, you're talking like a Consie."

I answered: "Why, so I am. That's terrible."

"Well," I replied, "I don't know about that. Maybe . . ."

"Yeah," I said thoughtfully. "Maybe . . ."

It's an axiom of my trade that things are invisible except against a contrasting background. Like, for instance, the opinions and attitudes of Fowler Schocken.

Humor me, Fowler, I thought. Keep me guarded. I don't want to run into an ambivalent fantasy like Hedy again, ever. The symbolism may have been obvious, but she hurt me bad with her symbolic little needle.

15

RUNSTEAD wasn't there when our little procession arrived in executives' country of the Schocken Tower. There were Fowler, me, Jack O'Shea, secretaries—and the weapons squads I had demanded.

Runstead's secretary said he was down the hall, and we waited . . . and waited . . . and waited. After an hour I suggested that he wasn't coming back. After another hour word got to us that a body had been found smashed flat on the first setback of the Tower, hundreds of feet below. It was very, very difficult to identify.

The secretary wept hysterically and opened Runstead's desk and safe. Eventually we found a diary covering the past few months of Runstead's life. Interspersed with details of his work, his amours, memos for future campaigns, notes on good out-of-the-way restaurants, and the like were entries that said: "He was here again last night. He told me to hit harder on the shock-appeal. He scares me . . . He says the Starrzelius campaign needed guts. He scares *hell* out of me. Understand he used to scare everybody in the old days when he was alive . . . GWH again last night . . . *Saw him by daylight* first time. Jumped and yelled but nobody noticed. Wish he'd go away . . . GWH teeth seem bigger, pointier today. I ought to get help . . . He said I'm no good, disgrace to profession . . ."

After a while we realized that "he" was the ghost of George Washington Hill, father of our profession, founder of the singing commercial, shock-value, and God knows what else.

"Poor fellow," said Schocken, white-faced. "Poor, poor fellow. If only I'd known. If only he'd come to me in time."

The last entry said raggedly: "Told me I'm no good. I know I'm no good. Unworthy of the profession. They all know it. Can see it in their faces.

Everybody knows it. He told them. Damn him. Damn him and his teeth. Damn—"

"Poor, poor fellow," said Schocken, almost sobbing. He turned to me and said: "You see? The strains of our profession . . ."

Sure I saw. A prefabricated diary and an unidentifiable splash of protoplasm. It might have been 180 pounds of Chicken Little down there on the first setback. But I would have been wasting my breath. I nodded soberly, humoring him.

I was restored to my job at the top of Venus Section. I saw Fowler's analyst daily. And I kept my armed guard. In tearful sessions the old man would say: "You must relinquish this symbol. It's all that stands between you and reality now, Mitch. Dr. Lawler tells me—"

Dr. Lawler told Fowler Schocken what I told Dr. Lawler. And that was the slow progress of my "integration." I hired a medical student to work out traumas for me backwards from the assumption that my time as a consumer had been a psychotic fugue, and he came up with some honeys. A few I had to veto as not quite consistent with my dignity, but there were enough left to make Dr. Lawler drop his pencil every once in a while. One by one we dug them up, and I have never been so bored in my life.

But one thing I would not surrender, and that was my insistence that my life and Fowler Schocken's life were in danger.

Fowler and I got closer and closer—a thing I've seen before. He thought he had made a convert. I was ashamed to string him along. He was being very good to me. But it was a matter of life or death. The rest was side show.

The day came when Fowler Schocken said

gently: "Mitch, I'm afraid heroic measures are in order. I don't ask you to dispense with this fence of yours against reality. But *I* am going to dismiss *my* guards."

"They'll kill you, Fowler!" burst from me.

He shook his head gently. "You'll see. I'm not afraid." Argument was quite useless. After a bit of it, acting on sound psychological principles, he told the lieutenant of his office squad: "I won't be needing you any more. Please report with your men to Plant Security Pool for reassignment. Thank you very much for your loyalty and attention to detail during these weeks."

The lieutenant saluted, but he and his men looked sick. They were going from an easy job in executives' country to lobby patrol or night detail or mail guard or messenger service at ungodly hours. They filed out, and I knew Fowler Schocken's hours were numbered.

That night he was garroted on his way home by somebody who had slugged his chauffeur and substituted himself at the pedals of the Fowler Schocken Cadillac. The killer, apparently, a near-moron, resisted arrest and was clubbed to death, giggling. His tattoo had been torn off; he was quite unidentifiable.

You can easily imagine how much work was done in the office the next day. There was a memorial Board meeting held and resolutions passed saying it was a dirty shame and a great profession never would forget and so on. Messages of condolence were sent by the other agencies, including Taunton's. I got some odd looks when I crumpled the Taunton message in my fist and used some very bad language. Commercial rivalry, after all, goes just so far. We're all gentlemen here, of course. A hard, clean fight and may the best agency win.

But no Board member paid it much mind. They all were thinking of just one thing: the Schocken block of voting shares.

Fowler Schocken Associates was capitalized at 7×10^{12} megabux, voting shares par at M\$^{2}0.1, giving us 7×10^{13} shares. Of these, 3.5×10^{13} $+$ 1 shares were purchasable only by employees holding AAAA labor contracts or better—roughly speaking, star class. The remaining shares by SEC order had been sold on the open market in order to clothe Fowler Schocken Associates with public interest. As customary, Fowler Schocken himself had through dummies snapped these up at the obscure stock exchanges where they had been put on sale.

In his own name he held a modest $.75 \times 10^{13}$ shares and distributed the rest with a lavish hand. I myself, relatively junior in spite of holding perhaps the number two job in the organization, had accumulated via bonuses and incentive pay only about $.857 \times 10^{12}$ shares. Top man around the Board table probably was Harvey Bruner. He was Schocken's oldest associate and had corralled $.83 \times 10^{13}$ shares over the years. (Nominally this gave him the bulge on Fowler —but he knew, of course, that in a challenge those other 3.5×10^{13} $+$ 1 shares would come rolling in on carloads of proxies, all backing Fowler with a mysterious unanimity. Besides, he was loyal.) He seemed to think he was heir-apparent, and some of the more naive Research and Development people were already sucking up to him, more fools they. He was an utterly uncreative, utterly honest wheel horse. Under his heavy hand the delicate thing that was Fowler Schocken Associates would disintegrate in a year.

If I were gambling, I would have given odds on Sillery, the Media chief, for copping the Schocken bloc and on down in descending order to myself, on whom I would have taken odds—long, long odds. That obviously was the way most of them felt, except the infatuated Bruner and a few dopes. You could tell. Sillery was surrounded by a respectful little court that doubtless remembered such remarks from Fowler as: "Media, gentlemen, is basic-basic!" and: "Media for brains, copysmiths for talent!" I was practically a leper at the end of the table, with my guards silently eyeing the goings-on. Sillery glanced at them once, and I could read him like a book: *"That's been going on long enough; we'll knock off that eccentric first thing."*

What we had been waiting for came about at last. "The gentlemen from the American Arbitration Association, Probate Section, are here, gentlemen."

They were of the funereal type, according to tradition. Through case-hardening or deficient senses of humor they refrained from giggling while Sillery gave them a measured little speech of welcome about their sad duty and how we wished we could meet them under happier circumstances and so on.

They read the will in a rapid mumble and passed copies around. The part I read first said: "To my dear friend and associate Mitchell Courtenay I bequeath and devise my ivory-inlaid oak finger-ring (inventory number 56,987) and my seventy-five shares of Sponsors' Stock in the Institute for the Diffusion of Psychoanalytic Knowledge, a New York Non-Profit Corporation, with the injunction that he devote his leisure hours to active participation in this organization and the furtherance of its noble aim." Well, Mitch, I told myself, you're through. I tossed the copy on the table and leaned back to take a swift rough inventory of my liquid assets.

"Hard lines, Mr. Courtenay," a brave and sympathetic research man I hardly knew told me. "Mr. Sillery seems pleased with himself."

I glanced at the bequest to Sillery—paragraph one. Sure enough, he got Fowler's personal shares and huge chunks of stock in Managerial Investment Syndicate, Underwriters Holding Corporation and a couple of others.

The research man studied my copy of the will. "If you don't mind my saying so, Mr. Courtenay," he told me, "the old man could have treated you better. I never heard of this outfit and I'm pretty familiar with the psychoanalytic field."

I seemed to hear Fowler chuckling nearby, and sat bolt upright. "Why the old so-and-so!" I gasped. It fitted like lock and key, with his bizarre sense of humor to oil the movement.

Sillery was clearing his throat and an instant silence descended on the Board room.

The great man spoke. "It's a trifle crowded here, gentlemen. I wish somebody would move that all persons other than Board members be asked to leave—"

I got up and said: "I'll save you the trouble, Sillery. Come on, boys. Sillery, I may be back." I and my guard left.

The Institute for the Diffusion of Psychoanalytic Knowledge, a New York Non-Profit Corporation, turned out to be a shabby three-room suite downtown in Yonkers. There was a weird old gal in the outer office pecking away at a typewriter. It was like something out of Dickens. A sagging rack held printed pamphlets with fly-specks on them.

"I'm from Fowler Schocken Associates," I told her.

She jumped. "Excuse me, sir! I didn't notice you. How is Mr. Schocken?"

I told her how he was, and she began to blubber. He was such a *good* man, giving so *generously* for the Cause. What on Earth would she and her poor brother ever do now? Poor Mr. Schocken! Poor her! Poor brother!

"All may not be lost," I told her. "Who's in charge here?" She sniffled that her brother was in the inner office. "Please break it to him gently, Mr. Courtenay. He's so delicate and sensitive—"

I said I would, and walked in. Brother was snoring-drunk, flopped over his desk. I joggled him awake, and he looked at me with a bleary and cynical eye. "Washawan?"

"I'm from Fowler Schocken Associates. I want to look at your books."

He shook his head emphatically. "Nossir. Only the old man himself gets to see the books."

"He's dead," I told him. "Here's the will." I showed him the paragraph and my identification.

"Well," he said. "The joy-ride's over. Or do you keep us going? You see what it says there, Mr. Courtenay? He enjoins you—"

"I see it," I told him. "The books, please."

He got them out of a surprising vault behind a plain door.

A mere three hours of backbreaking labor over them showed me that the Institute was in existence solely for holding and voting 56 per cent of the stock of an outfit called General Phosphate Reduction Corporation of Newark according to the whims of Fowler Schocken.

I went out into the corridor and said to my guards: "Come on, boys. Newark next."

I won't bore you with the details. It was single-tracked for three stages and then it split. One of the tracks ended two stages later in the Frankfort Used Machine Tool Brokerage Company, which voted 32 per cent of the Fowler Schocken Associates "public sale" stock. The other track forked again one stage later and wound up eventually in United Concessions Corp. and Waukegan College of Dentistry and Orthodontia, which voted the remainder.

Two weeks later on Board morning I walked into the Board room with my guards.

Sillery was presiding. He looked haggard and worn, as though he'd been up all night every night for the past couple of weeks looking for something.

"Courtenay!" he snarled. "I thought you understood that you were to leave your regiment outside!"

I nodded to honest, dumb old Harvey Bruner, whom I'd let in on it. Loyal to Schocken, loyal to me, he bleated: "Mr. Chairman, I move that members be permitted to admit company plant-protection personnel assigned to them in such number as they think necessary for their bodily protection."

"Second the motion, Mr. Chairman," I said. "Bring them in, boys, will you?" My guards, grinning, began to lug in transfer cases full of proxies to me.

Eyes popped and jaws dropped as the pile mounted. It took a long time for them to be counted and authenticated. The final vote stood: For, 5.73×10^{13}; against, 1.27×10^{13}. All the Against votes were Sillery's and Sillery's alone. There were no abstentions. The others jumped to my side like cats on a griddle.

Loyal old Harve moved that chairmanship of the meeting be transferred to me, and it was carried unanimously. He then moved that Sillery be pensioned off, his shares of voting stock to be purchased at par by the firm and deposited in the bonus fund. Carried unanimously. Then—a slash of the whip just to remind them—he moved that one Thomas Heatherby, a junior Art man who had sucked up outrageously to Sillery, be downgraded from Board level and deprived without compensation of his minute block of voting shares. Carried unanimously. Heatherby didn't even dare scream about it. Half a loaf is better than none, he may have said to himself, choking down his anger.

It was done. I was master of Fowler Schocken Associates. And I had learned to despise everything for which it stood.

16

"FLASH-FLASH, Mr. Courtenay," said my secretary's voice. I hit the GA button.

"Consie arrested Albany on neighbor's denunciation. Shall I line it up?"

"God-damn it!" I exploded. "How many times do I have to give you standing orders? Of course you line it up. Why the hell not?"

She quavered: "I'm sorry, Mr. Courtenay—I thought it was kind of far out—"

"Stop thinking, then. Arrange the transportation." Maybe I shouldn't have been so rough on her—but I wanted to find Kathy, if I had to turn every Consie cell in the country upside down to do it. I had driven Kathy into hiding—out of fear that I would turn her in—now I wanted to get her back.

An hour later I was in the Upstate Mutual Protective Association's HQ. They were a local outfit that had a lot of contracts in the area, including Albany. Their board chairman himself met me and my guards at the elevator. "An honor," he burbled. "A great, great honor, Mr. Courtenay, and what may I do for you?"

"My secretary asked you not to get to work on your Consie suspect until I arrived. Did you?"

"Of course not, Mr. Courtenay! Some of the employees may have roughed him up a little, informally, but he's in quite good shape."

"I want to see him."

He led the way anxiously. He was hoping to get in a word that might grow into a cliency with Fowler Schocken Associates, but he was afraid to speak up.

The suspect was sitting on a stool under the usual dazzler. He was a white-collar consumer of thirty or so. He had a couple of bruises on his face.

"Turn that thing off," I said.

A square-faced foreman said: "But we always—" One of my guards, without wasting words, shoved him aside and switched off the dazzler.

"It's all right, Lombardo," the board chairman said hastily. "You're to co-operate with these gentlemen."

"Chair," I said, and sat down facing the suspect. I told him: "My name's Courtenay. What's yours?"

He looked at me with pupils that were beginning to expand again. "Fillmore," he said, precisely. "August Fillmore. Can you tell me what all this is about?"

"You're suspected of being a Consie."

There was a gasp from all the UMPA people in the room. I was violating the most elementary principle of jurisprudence by informing the accused of the nature of his crime. I knew all about that, and didn't give a damn.

"Completely ridiculous," Fillmore spat. "I'm a

respectable married man with eight children and another coming along. Who on earth told you people such nonsense?"

"Tell him who," I said to the board chairman.

He stared at me, goggle-eyed, unable to believe what he had heard. "Mr. Courtenay," he said at last, "with all respect, I can't take the responsibility for such a thing! It's quite unheard of. The entire body of law respecting the rights of informers—"

"I'll take the responsibility. Do you want me to put it in writing?"

"No, no, no, no, no! Nothing like that! Please, Mr. Courtenay—suppose I tell the informer's name to you, understanding that you know the law and are a responsible person—and then I leave the room?"

"Any way you want to do it is all right with me."

He grinned placatingly, and whispered in my ear: "A Mrs. Worley. The two families share a room. Please be careful, Mr. Courtenay—"

"Thanks," I said. He gathered eyes like a hostess and nervously retreated with his employees.

"Well, Fillmore," I told the suspect, "he says it's Mrs. Worley."

He began to swear, and I cut him off. "I'm a busy man," I said. "You know your goose is cooked, of course. You know what Vogt says on the subject of conservation?"

The name apparently meant nothing to him. "Who's that?" he asked distractedly.

"Never mind. Let's change subjects. I have a lot of money. I can set up a generous pension for your family while you're away if you co-operate and admit you're a Consie."

He thought hard for a few moments and then said: "Sure I'm a Consie. What of it? Guilty or innocent, I'm sunk so why not say so?"

"If you're a red-hot Consie, suppose you quote me some passages from Osborne?"

He had never heard of Osborne, and slowly began to fake: "Well, there's the one that starts: 'A Consie's first duty, uh, is to, to prepare for a general uprising—' I don't remember the rest, but that's how it starts."

"Pretty close," I told him. "Now how about your cell meetings? Who-all's there?"

"I don't know them by name," he said more glibly. "We go by numbers. There's a dark-haired fellow, he's the boss, and, uh—"

It was a remarkable performance. It certainly, however, had nothing to do with the semi-mythical Conservationist heroes, Vogt and Osborne, whose books were required reading in all cells—when copies could be found.

We left.

I told the board chairman, hovering anxiously outside in the corridor: "I don't think he's a Consie."

I was president of Fowler Schocken Associates and he was only the board chairman of a jerkwater local police outfit, but *that* was too much. He drew himself up and said with dignity: "We administer justice, Mr. Courtenay. And an ancient, basic tenet of justice is: 'Better that one thousand innocents suffer unjustly than one guilty person be permitted to escape.'"

"I am aware of the maxim," I said. "Good day."

My instrument corporal went *boing* as the crash-crash priority signal sounded in his ear and handed me the phone. It was my secretary back in Schocken Tower, reporting another arrest, this one in Pile City Three, off Cape Cod.

We flew out to Pile City Three, which was rippling that day over a long, swelling sea. I hate the Pile Cities—as I've said, I suffer from motion sickness.

This Consie suspect turned out to be a professional criminal. He had tried a smash-and-grab raid on a jewelry store, intending to snatch a trayful of oak and mahogany pins, leaving behind a lurid note all about Consie vengeance and beware of the coming storm when the Consies take over and kill all the rich guys. It was intended to throw off suspicion.

He was very stupid.

It was a Burns-protected city, and I had a careful chat with their resident manager. He admitted first that most of their Consie arrests during the past month or so had been like that, and then admitted that *all* their Consie arrests for the past month or so had been like that. Formerly they had broken up authentic Consie cells at the rate of maybe one a week. He thought maybe it was a seasonal phenomenon.

From there we went back to New York, where another Consie had been picked up. I saw him and listened to him rant for a few minutes. He was posted on Consie theory and could quote you Vogt and Osborne by the page. He also asserted that God had chosen him to wipe the wastrels from the face of Mother Earth. He said of course he was in the regular Consie organization, but he would die before he gave up any of its secrets. And I knew he certainly would, because he didn't know any. The Consies wouldn't have accepted anybody that unstable if they were down to three members with one sinking fast.

We went back to Schocken Tower at sunset, and my guard changed. It had been a lousy day. It had been, as far as results were concerned, a carbon copy of all the days I had spent since I inherited the agency.

There was a meeting scheduled. I didn't want to go, but my conscience troubled me when I thought of the pride and confidence Fowler Schocken must have felt in me when he made me his heir. Before I dragged myself to the Board room I checked with a special detail I had set up in the Business Espionage section.

"Nothing, sir," my man said. "No leads whatsoever on your—on Dr. Nevin. The tracer we had on the Chlorella personnel man petered out. Uh, shall we keep trying—?"

"Keep trying," I said. "If you need a bigger appropriation or more investigators, don't hesitate. Do me a real job."

He swore loyalty and hung up, probably thinking that the boss was an old fool, mooning over a wife—not even permanently married to him—who had decided to slip out of the picture. What he made out of the others I had asked him to trace, I didn't know. All I knew was that they had vanished, all my few contacts with the Consies picked up in Costa Rica, the sewers of New York, and on the Moon. Kathy had never come back to her apartment or the hospital, Warren Astron had never returned to his sucker-trap on Shopping One, my Chlorella cellmates had vanished into the jungle—and so it went, all down the line.

Board meeting.

"Sorry to be late, gentlemen. I'll dispense with

188

opening remarks. Charlie, how's Research and Development doing on the Venus question?"

He got up. "Mr. Courtenay, gentlemen, in my humble way I think I can say, informally, that R. and D. is in there punching and that my boys are a credit to Fowler Schocken Associates. Specifically, we've licked the greenhouse effect. *Quantitatively.* Experiments in vitro have confirmed the predictions of our able physical chemistry and thermodynamics section based on theory and math. A CO_2 blanket around Venus at forty thousand feet, approximately .05 feet thick, will be self-sustaining and self-regulating, and will moderate surface temperatures some five degrees a year, steadying at eighty to eighty-five degrees. We're exploring now the various ways this enormous volume of gas can be obtained and hurled at high velocity into the stratosphere of Venus. Considered broadly, we can find the CO_2, or manufacture it, or both. I say, find it. Volcanic activity is present, but your typical superficial Venus eruption would seem to be liquid NH_4 compressed by gravity in crevices until it seeps to a weaker formation through faults and porous rock and then blows its top. We are certain, however, that deep drilling would tap considerable reservoirs of liquid CO_2—"

"How certain?" I asked.

"Quite certain, Mr. Courtenay," he said, hardly able to suppress the you-couldn't-be-expected-to-understand smile that technical people give you. "Phase-rule analysis of the O'Shea reports—"

I interrupted again. "Would you go to Venus on the strength of that certainty, other things being equal?"

"Certainly," he said, a little offended. "Shall I go into the technical details?"

"No thanks, Charlie. Continue as before."

"Hrrmp. So—at present we are wrapping up the green-house-effect phase in two respects. We are preparing a maximum-probability map of drilling sites, and we are designing a standard machine for unattended deep drilling. My policy on the design is cheapness, self-power, and remote control. I trust this is satisfactory?"

"Very much so. Thank you, Charlie. One point, though. If the stuff is there and if it's abundant, we have a prospect of trouble. If it's *too* abundant and easy to get at, it might become feasible for Venus to export liquid CO_2 to Earth—which we definitely do not want. CO_2 is in good supply here, and no purpose would be served by underselling the earthside producers of it. Let's bear in mind always that Venus is going to pay its way with raw materials in short supply on Earth, and is not going to compete pricewise with the mother planet. Iron, yes. Nitrates, emphatically yes. We'll pay them a good enough price for such things to keep them buying earthside products and enable them to give earthside bankers, insurance companies, and carrying trade their business. But never forget that Venus is there for us to exploit, and don't ever get it turned around. I want you, Charlie, to get together with Auditing and determine whether tapping underground CO_2 pools will ever make it possible for Venus to deliver CO_2 F.O.B. New York at a competitive price. If it does, your present plans are *out*. You'll have to get your greenhouse-effect blanketing gas by manufacturing it in a more expensive way."

"Right, Mr. Courtenay," Charlie said, scribbling busily.

"Right. Does anybody else have anything special on the Venus program before we go on?"

Bernhard, our comptroller, stuck his hand up, and I nodded.

"Question about Mr. O'Shea," he rumbled. "We're carrying him as a consultant at a very healthy figure. I've been asking around—and I hope I haven't been going offside, Mr. Courtenay, but it's my job—I've been asking around and I find that we've been getting damn-all consultation from him. Also, I should mention that he's drawn heavily in recent weeks on retainers not yet due. If we canned—if we severed our connection with him at this time, he'd be owing us money. Also—well, this is trivial, but it gives you an idea. The girls in my department are complaining about his annoying them."

My eyebrows went up. "I think we should hang onto him for whatever prestige rubs off, Ben, though his vogue does seem to be passing. Give him an argument about further advances. And as for the girls—well, I'm surprised. I thought they didn't complain when he made passes at them."

"Seen him lately?" grunted Bernhard.

No; I realized I hadn't.

The rest of the meeting went fast.

Back in my office I asked my night-shift secretary whether O'Shea was in the building, and if so to send for him.

He came in smelling of liquor and complaining loudly. "Damn it, Mitch, enough is enough! I just stepped in to pick up one of the babes for the night and you grab me. Aren't you taking this consultation thing too seriously? You've got my name to use; what more do you want?"

He looked like hell. He looked like a miniature of the fat, petulant, shabby Napoleon I at Elba. But a moment after he had come in I suddenly couldn't think of anything but Kathy. It took me a moment to figure out.

"Well?" he demanded. "What are you staring at? Isn't my lipstick on straight?"

The liquor covered it up some, but a little came through: *Ménage à Deux,* the perfume I'd had created for Kathy and Kathy alone when we were in Paris, the stuff she loved and sometimes used too much of. I could hear her saying: "I can't help it, darling; it's *so* much nicer than formalin, and that's what I usually smell of after a day at the hospital . . ."

"Sorry, Jack," I said evenly. "I didn't know it was your howling-night. It'll keep. Have fun."

He grimaced and left, almost waddling on his short legs.

I grabbed my phone and slammed a connection through to my special detail in Business Espionage. "Put tails on Jack O'Shea," I snapped. "He's leaving the building soon. Tail him and tail everybody he contacts. Night and day. If I hit paydirt on this you and your men get upgraded and bonused. But God help you if you pull a butch."

17

I GOT SO NO-
body dared to come near me. I couldn't help myself.
I was living for one thing only: the daily reports
from the tails on O'Shea. Anything else I tried to
handle bored and irritated me to distraction.

After a week there were twenty-four tails working at a time on O'Shea and people with whom
he had talked. They were headwaiters, his lecture agent, girls, an old test-pilot friend of his
stationed at Astoria, a cop he got into a drunken
argument with one night—but was he really drunk
and was it really an argument?—and other unsur-
prising folk.

One night, quietly added to the list was: "Consumer, female, about 30, 5′4″, 102 lbs., redhead,
eyes not seen, cheaply dressed. Subject entered
Hash Heaven (restaurant) 1837 after waiting 14
minutes outside and went immediately to table
waited on by new contact, which table just vacated by party. Conjecture: subject primarily interested in waitress. Ordered hash, ate very lightly,
exchanged few words with contact. Papers may

have been passed but impossible to observe at tailing distance. Female operative has picked up contact."

About thirty, five-four, one-twenty. It could be. I phoned to say: "Bear down on that one. Rush me everything new that you get. How about finding out more from the restaurant?"

Business Espionage began to explain, with embarrassment, that they'd do it if I insisted, but that it wasn't good technique. Usually the news got to the person being tailed and—"

"Okay," I said. "Do it your way."

"Hold it a minute, Mr. Courtenay, please. Our girl just checked in—the new contact went home to the Taunton Building. She has Stairs 17–18 on the Thirty-fifth floor."

"What's the thirty-fifth?" I asked, heavy-hearted.

"For couples."

"Is she—?"

"She's unattached, Mr. Courtenay. Our girl pretended to apply for the vacancy. They told her Mrs. 17 is holding 18 for the arrival of her husband. He's upstate harvesting."

"What time do the stairs close at Taunton's?" I demanded.

"2200, Mr. Courtenay."

I glanced at my desk clock. "Call your tail off her," I said. "That's all for now."

I got up and told my guards: "I'm going out without you, gentlemen. Please wait here. Lieutenant, can I borrow your gun?"

"Of course, Mr. Courtenay." He passed over a .25 UHV. I checked the magazine and went out on foot, alone.

As I left the lobby of Schocken Tower a shadowy young man detached himself from the wall and drifted after me. I crossed him up by walking in the deserted street, a dark, narrow slit between the mighty midtown buildings. Monoxide and smog hung heavily in the unconditioned air, but I had antisoot plugs. He did not. I heard him wheeze at a respectable distance behind me. An occasional closed cab whizzed past us, the driver puffing and drawn as he pumped the pedals.

Without looking back I turned the corner of Schocken Tower and instantly flattened against the wall. My shadow drifted past and stopped in consternation, peering into the gloom.

I slammed the long barrel of the pistol against the back of his neck in a murderous rabbit punch and walked on. He was probably one of my own men; but I didn't want anybody's men along.

I got to the Taunton Building's night-dweller entrance at 2159. Behind me the timelock slammed the door. There was an undersized pay elevator. I dropped in a quarter, punched 35, and read notices while it creaked upward. "NIGHT-DWELLERS ARE RESPONSIBLE FOR THEIR OWN POLICING. MANAGEMENT ASSUMES NO RESPONSIBILITY FOR THEFTS, ASSAULTS, OR RAPES." "NIGHT DWELLERS WILL NOTE THAT BARRIERS ARE UPPED AT 2210 NIGHTLY AND ARRANGE THEIR CALLS OF NATURE ACCORDINGLY." "RENT IS DUE AND PAYABLE NIGHTLY IN ADVANCE AT THE AUTOCLERK." "MANAGEMENT RESERVES THE RIGHT TO REFUSE RENTAL TO PATRONS OF STARRZELIUS PRODUCTS."

The door opened on the stairwell of the thirty-fifth floor. It was like looking into a maggoty cheese. People, men and women, squirming uneasily, trying to find some comfort before the barriers upped. I looked at my watch and saw: 2208.

I picked my way carefully and very, very slowly in the dim light over and around limbs and torsos, with many apologies, counting . . . at the seventeenth step I stepped over a huddled figure as my watch said: 2210.

With a rusty clank, the barriers upped, cutting off steps seventeen and eighteen, containing me and—

She sat up, looking scared and angry, with a small pistol in her hand.

"Kathy," I said.

She dropped the pistol. "Mitch. You fool." Her voice was low and urgent. "What are you doing here? They haven't given up, they're still out to murder you—"

"I know all that," I said. "I'm grandstanding, Kathy. I'm putting my head into the lion's mouth to show you I mean it when I say that you're right and I was wrong."

"How did you find me?" she asked suspiciously.

"Some of your perfume came off on O'Shea. *Ménage à Deux.*"

She looked around at the cramped quarters and giggled. "It certainly is, isn't it?"

"The heat's off, Kathy," I told her. "I'm not just here to paw you, with or without your consent. I'm here to tell you that I'm on your side. Name it and you can have it."

She looked at me narrowly and asked: "Venus?"

"It's yours."

"Mitch," she said, "if you're lying—if you're lying—"

"You'll know by tomorrow if we get out of here alive. Until then there's nothing more to be said about it, is there? We're in for the night."

"Yes," she said. "We're in for the night." And

then, suddenly, passionately: "God, how I've missed you!"

Wake-up whistles screamed at 0600. They were loaded with skull-rattling subsonics, just to make sure that no slugabeds would impede the morning evacuation.

Kathy began briskly to stow away the bedding in the stairs. "Barriers down in five minutes," she snapped. She lifted Stair seventeen's lid and fished around in it for a flat box that opened into a make-up kit. "Hold still."

I yelped as a razor raked across the top of my right eyebrow. "Hold—*still!*" R-R-R-R-ip! It cut a swathe across my left eyebrow. Briskly she touched my face here and there with mysterious brushes.

"Flup!" I said as she turned up my upper lip and tucked a pledget of plastic under it. Two gummy wads pasted my ears against my head and she said: "There," and showed me the mirror.

"Good," I told her. "I got out of here once in the morning rush. I think we can do it again."

"There go the barriers," she said tensely, hearing some preliminary noise that was lost on my inexperienced ear.

The barriers clanged down. We were the only night-dwellers left on the thirty-fifth floor. But we were not alone. B. J. Taunton and two of his boys stood there. Taunton was swaying a little on his feet, red-faced and grinning. Each of his boys had a machine pistol trained on me.

Taunton hiccuped and said: "This was a hell of an unfortunate place for you to go chippy-chasing, Courtenay, ol' man. We have a photo-register for gate-crashers like you. Girlie, if you will kindly step aside—"

She didn't step aside. She stepped right into Taunton's arms, jamming her gun against his navel. His red face went the color of putty. "You know what to do," she said grimly.

"Boys," he said faintly, "drop the guns. For God's sake, drop them!"

They exchanged looks. *"Drop them!"* he begged.

They took an eternity to lay down their machine pistols, but they did. Taunton began to sob.

"Turn your backs," I told them, "and lie down." I had my borrowed UHV out. It felt wonderful.

The elevator could too easily have been flooded with gas. We walked down the stairs. It was a long, slow, careful business, though all night-dwellers had been cleared hours ago for B.J.'s coup. He sobbed and babbled all the way. At the tenth-floor landing he wailed: "I've got to have a drink, Courtenay. I'm dying. There's a bar right here, you can keep that gun on me—"

Kathy laughed humorlessly at the idea, and we continued our slow step-by-step progress.

At the night-dweller exit I draped my coat over Kathy's gun hand in spite of the winter outside. "It's all right!" B.J. called quaveringly to an astounded lobby guard who started our way. "These people are friends of mine. It's quite all right!"

We walked with him to the shuttlemouth and dived in, leaving him, gray-faced and sweating, in the street. It was safety in numbers. The only way he could get at us was by blowing up the entire shuttle, and he wasn't equipped for it. We zigzagged for an hour, and I called my office from a station phone. A plant protection detail rendezvoused with us at another station, and we were in the Schocken Tower fifteen minutes later.

A morning paper gave us our only laugh so far

that day. It said, among other things, that a coolant leak had been detected at 0300 today in the stairwell of the Taunton Building. B. J. Taunton himself, at the risk of his life, had supervised the evacuation of the Taunton Building night-dwellers in record time and without casualties.

Over a tray breakfast on my desk I told Kathy: "Your hair looks like hell. Does that stuff wash out?"

"Enough of this lovemaking," she said. "You told me I could have Venus. Mitch, I meant it. And Venus by-God belongs to us. We're the only people who know what to do with it and also we landed the first man there. O'Shea is one of us, Mitch."

"Since when?"

"Since his mother and father found he wasn't growing, that's since when. They knew the W.C.A. was going to need space-pilots soon—and the smaller the better. Earth didn't discover Venus. The W.C.A. did. And we demand the right to settle it. Can you deliver?"

"Sure," I said. "God, it's going to be a headache. We have our rosters filled now—eager suckers itching to get to Venus and be exploited by and for the Earth and Fowler Schocken. Well, I'll backtrack."

I punched the intercom to R. & D. "Charlie!" I said. "About the CO_2 competition with Earth producers. Forget about it. I've found that Taunton's bills most of the makers."

"Sure, Mr. Courtenay," Charlie said happily. "The preliminary work looks as if we'll give them a real kick in the groin."

I said to Kathy: "Can you bring Runstead back to life for me? I don't know where the W.C.A.

199

has been holding him, but we need him here. This is going to be a job. A copysmith's highest art is to convince people without letting them know that they're being convinced. What I've got to do is make my copysmiths unconvince people without letting either the copysmiths or the people know what I'm doing to them. I can use some high-grade help that I can talk freely to."

"It can be arranged," she said, kissing me lightly. "That's for saying 'We.' "

"Huh?" I said. "Did I say 'we'?" Then I understood. "Oh. Look, darling, I've got a dandy executive's living suite, twelve by twelve, upstairs. You had a hard night. Suppose you head upstairs and cork off for a while. I've got a lot of work to do."

She kissed me again and said: "Don't work too hard, Mitch. I'll see you tonight."

18

I COULDN'T HAVE done it without Runstead—not in time. He came whistling back from Chi, where he'd been holed up since he pretended suicide, in response to an underground message from Kathy. He arrived in the middle of a Board meeting; we shook hands and the Board cheerfully swallowed the story that he'd dropped out of sight to do some secret work. After all, they'd swallowed it once before. He knew what the job was; he sank his teeth in it.

Consie or no Consie, I still thought Runstead was a rat.

But I had to admit things were leaping.

On the surface level, Fowler Schocken Associates had launched a giant all-client slogan contest, with fifteen hundred first prizes—all of them a berth on the Venus rocket. There were eight hundred thousand prizes in all, but the others didn't matter. Judging was turned over to an impartial firm of contest analyzers, which turned out to be headed by the brother-in-law of a friend of Runstead's. Only fourteen hundred of the prize winners, Matt told me, were actually members of the Consie underground. The other hundred were dummy names entirely, to take care of last minute emergencies.

I took Kathy with me to Washington to spark the final clearance of the rocket for flight, while Runstead minded the baby back in New York. I'd been in Washington often enough for a luncheon or an afternoon, but this was going to be a two-day job; I looked forward to it like a kid. I parked Kathy at the hotel and made her promise not to do any solo sight-seeing, then caught a cab to the State Department. A morose little man in a bowler hat was waiting in the anteroom; when he heard my name he got up hastily and offered me his seat. Quite a change from the Chlorella days, Mitch, old boy, I told myself. Our attaché came flustering out to greet me; I calmed him and explained what I wanted.

"Easiest thing in the world, Mr. Courtenay," he promised. "I'll get the enabling bill put through committee this afternoon, and with any luck at all it'll clear both houses tonight."

I said expansively, "Fine. Need any backing?"

"Oh, I don't think so, Mr. Courtenay. Might be nice for you to address the House in the morning, if you can find the time. They'd love to hear from you, and it would smooth things over a little for a quick passage."

"Glad to," I said, reaching down for my bag. The man in the bowler hat beat me to it and handed it to me with a little bow. "Just set your time, Abels," I told the legate. "I'll be there."

"Thank you very *much,* Mr. Courtenay!" He opened the door for me. The little man said tentatively:

"Mr. Abels?"

The legate shook his head. "You can see how busy I am," he said, not unkindly. "Come back tomorrow."

The little man smiled gratefully and followed me out the door. We both hailed a cab, and he opened the door for me. You know what cabs are like in Washington. "Can I drop you anywhere?" I asked.

"It's very good of you," he said, and followed me in. The driver leaned back on his pedals and looked in at us.

I told him: "The Park Starr for me. But drop the other gentleman off first."

"Sure." The driver nodded. "White House, Mr. President?"

"Yes, please," said the little man. "I can't tell you how pleased I am to meet you, Mr. Courtenay," he went on. "I overheard your conversation

202

with Mr. Abels, you know. It was very interesting to hear that the Venus rocket is so near completion. Congress has pretty well got out of the habit of keeping me posted on what's going on. Of course, I know they're busy with their investigations and all. But—" He smiled. Mischievously, he said: "I entered your contest, Mr. Courtenay. My slogan was, 'I'm starry-eyed over Starrs, verily I am.' I don't suppose I could have gone along though, even if I'd won."

I said very sincerely: "I can't see how it would have been possible." And, a little less sincerely, "Besides, they must keep you pretty busy right here."

"Oh, not particularly. January's heavy; I convene Congress, you see, and they read me the State of the Union message. But the rest of the year passes slowly. Will you really address Congress tomorrow, Mr. Courtenay? It would mean a joint session, and they usually let me come for that."

"Be delighted to have you," I said cordially.

The little man had a warm smile, glinting through his glasses. The cab stopped and the President shook my hand warmly and got out. He poked his head in the door. "Uh," he said, looking apprehensively at the driver, "you've been swell. I may be stepping out of line in saying this, but if I might make a suggestion—I understand something about astronomy, it's a kind of hobby, and I hope you won't delay the ship's take-off past the present conjunction."

I stared. Venus was within ten degrees of opposition and was getting farther away—not that it mattered, since most of the trip would be coasting anyhow.

He held a finger to his lips. "Good-bye, sir,"

he said. I spent the rest of the trip staring at the backs of the driver's hairy ears, and wondering what the little man had been driving at.

We took the evening off, Kathy and I, to see the sights. I wasn't too much impressed. The famous cherry blossoms were beautiful, all right, but, with my new-found Conservationist sentiments, I found them objectionably ostentatious. "A dozen would have been plenty," I objected. "Scattering them around in vase after vase this way is a plain waste of the taxpayer's money. You know what they'd cost in Tiffany's?"

Kathy giggled. "Mitch, Mitch," she said. "Wait till we take over Venus. Did you ever think of what it's going to be like to have a whole *planet* to grow things in? Acres and acres of flowers—trees —everything?"

A plump schoolteacher-type leaning on the railing beside us straightened up, glared, sniffed, and walked away. "You're giving us a bad name," I told Kathy. "Before you get us in trouble, let's go to—let's go back to the hotel."

I woke up to an excited squeal from Kathy. "Mitch," she was saying from the bathroom, two round eyes peering wonderingly over the towel that was draped around her, "they've got a *tub* here! I opened the door to the shower stall, and it wasn't a stall at all! Can I, Mitch? Please?"

There are times when even an honest conservationist finds pleasure in being the acting head of Fowler Schocken Associates. I yawned and blew her a kiss and said, "Sure. And—make it all fresh water, hear?"

Kathy pretended to faint, but I noticed that she

wasted no time calling room service. While the tub was filling I dressed. We breakfasted comfortably and strolled to the Capitol hand in hand.

I found Kathy a seat in the pressbox and headed for the floor of the House. Our Washington lobby chief pushed through the crowd to me. He handed me a strip of facsimile paper. "It's all here, Mr. Courtenay," he said. "Uh—is everything all right?"

"Everything's just fine," I told him. I waved him off and looked at the facsimile. It was from Dicken, on the scene at the rocket:

> Passengers and crew alerted and on standby. First movement into ships begins at 1145 EST, loading completed by 1645 EST. Ship fully fueled, supplied, and provisioned since 0915. Security invoked but MIA, CIC, and Time-Life known to have filed coded dispatches through dummies. Chartroom asks please remind you: Takeoff possible only in AM hours.

I rubbed the tape between my palms; it disintegrated into ash. As I climbed to the podium, someone tugged at my elbow. It was the President, leaning out of his ceremonial box. "Mr. Courtenay," he whispered, his smile masklike on his face, "I guess you understood what I was trying to tell you yesterday in the cab. I'm glad the rocket's ready. And—" he widened his grin and bobbed his head in the precise manner of a statesman exchanging inconsequentialities with a distinguished visitor, "you probably know this, but —he's here."

I had no chance to find out who "he" was. As

the Speaker of the House came toward me hand outstretched and the applause started from the floor, I forced a smile to my face. But it was a trick of the rictus muscles entirely. I had little to smile about, if the news about the Venus rocket had trickled down to the President.

Fowler Schocken was a pious old hypocrite and Fowler Schocken was a grinning fraud, but if it hadn't been for Fowler Schocken I could never have got through that speech. I could hear his voice in my ears: "Sell 'em, Mitch; you can sell them if you'll keep in mind that they *want* to buy." And I sold the assembled legislators precisely what they wanted to own. I touched briefly on American enterprise and the home; I offered them a world to loot and a whole plunderable universe beyond it, once Fowler Schocken's brave pioneers had opened the way for it; I gave them a picture of assembly-line planets owned and operated by our very selves, the enterprising American businessmen who had made civilization great. They loved it. The applause was fantastic.

As the first waves died down, there were a dozen standing figures in the hall, clapping their hands and begging the chair for recognition. I hardly noticed; astonishingly, Kathy was gone from the pressbox. The Speaker selected white-haired old Colbee, lean and dignified with his four decades of service.

"The chair recognizes the gentleman from Yummy-Cola."

"Thank you very much, Mr. Speakuh." Colbee's face wore a courtly smile; but his eyes seemed to me the eyes of a snake. Yummy-Cola was nominally one of the few big independents; but I remembered that Fowler had commented once on their captive agency's surprising closeness to Taunton. "If I may ventuah to speak for the Upper Chamber, I should like to thank ouah distinguished guest for his very well-chosen remarks heah. I am certain that we all have enjoyed listening to a man of his calibeh and standing." Go back to the Berlitz school, you Westchester phony, I thought bitterly. I could feel the wienie coming as Colbee rumbled on. "With the permission of the chair, I should like to ask ouah guest a number of questions involving the legislation we have been asked to consider heah today." *Consider* indeed, you bastard, I thought. By now even the galleries had caught on to what was happening. I hardly needed to hear the rest:

"It may have escaped youah attention, but we are fortunate in having with us another guest. I refer of course to Mr. Taunton." He waved gracefully to the visitor's gallery, where B.J.'s red face appeared between two solid figures that I should have recognized at the first moment as his bodyguards. "In a brief discussion before ouah meeting heah, Mr. Taunton was good enough to give me some information which I would like Mr. Co'tenay to comment upon. First—" the snake eyes were steel now, "I would ask Mr. Co'tenay if the name of George Groby, wanted for Contract Breach and Femicide, is familiar to him. Second, I would like to ask if Mr. Co'tenay *is* Mr. Groby. Third, I would like to ask Mr. Co'tenay if there is any truth to the repo't, given me in confidence by someone in whom Mr. Taunton assures me I can repose absolute trust, that Mr. Co'tenay is a membeh in good standing of the World Conservation Association, known to most of us who are loyal Amurricans as—"

Even Colbee himself could not have heard the last words of his sentence. The uproar was like a physical blast.

19

SEEN IN RETRO-spect, everything that happened in the next wild quarter of an hour blurs and disappears like the shapes in a spinning kaleidoscope. But I remember tableaux, frozen moments of time that seem almost to have no relation to each other:

The waves of contempt and hatred that flowed around me, the contorted face of the President below me, screaming something unheard to the sound engineer in his cubicle, the wrathful eyes of the Speaker as he reached out for me.

Then the wild motion halted as the President's voice roared through the chamber at maximum amplification: "I declare this meeting adjourned!" —and the stunned expressions of the legislators at his unbelievable temerity. There was greatness in that little man. Before anyone could move or think he clapped his hands—the magnified report was like atomic fission—and a smartly uniformed squad moved in on us. "Take him away," the President declaimed, with a magnificent gesture, and at double-time the squad surrounded me and hustled me off the podium. The President convoyed us as far as the door while the assembly gathered its wits. His face was white with fear, but he whispered: "I can't make it stick, but it'll take them all afternoon to get a ruling from the C of C. God bless you, Mr. Courtenay."

And he turned back to face them. I do not think Caligula's Christians walked more courageously into the arena.

The guards were the President's own, honor men from Brink's leadership academy. The lieutenant said never a word to me, but I could read the controlled disgust on his face as he read the slip of paper the President had handed him. I knew he didn't like what he was ordered to do, and I knew he would do it.

They got me to Anacostia and put me on the President's own transport; they stayed with me and fed me, and one of them played cards with me, as the jets flared outside the ports and we covered territory. All they would not do was talk to me.

It was a long flight in that clumsy old luxury liner that "tradition" gave the President. Time had been wasted at the airport, and below us I could see the fuzzy band of the terminator creeping past. As we came down for a landing, it was full dark. And the waiting was not yet over, nor the wondering if Kathy had got out all right too and when I would see her again. The lieutenant left the ship alone; he was gone for a long, long time.

I spent the time kicking questions around in my mind—questions that had occurred to me before, but which I had dismissed. Now, with all the time in the world, and a future full of ifs, I took them out and looked them over.

For instance:

Kathy and Matt Runstead and Jack O'Shea had plotted together to put me on ice literally. All right, that accounted for most of the things that puzzled me. But it didn't account for Hester. And, when you stopped to think of it, it didn't account for all of Runstead's work, either.

The Consies were in favor of space travel. But Runstead had sabotaged the Venus test in Cal-Mex. There was no doubt of that; I had as good as a confession from his fall-guy. Could it have been a double cross? Runstead posing as a Consie who was posing as a copysmith, and in reality what?

I began wishing for Kathy for a completely new reason.

When the lieutenant came back it was midnight. "All right," he said to me. "A cab's waiting for you outside. The runner knows where to go."

I climbed out and stretched. "Thanks," I said awkwardly.

The lieutenant spat neatly on the ground between my feet. The door slammed, and I scrambled out of the way of the take-off.

The cab-runner was Mexican. I tried him on a question; no English. I tried again in my Chlorella U. Spanish; he gaped at me. There were fifty good reasons why I didn't want to go along with him without a much better idea of what was up.

But when I stopped to think of it, I had damn-all choice. The lieutenant had followed his orders. Now the orders were complied with, and I could see his active little military mind framing the report that would tip someone off to where they could find the notorious Consie, Mitchell Courtenay.

I would be a sitting duck; it would depend on whether Taunton or the police got to me first. It was not a choice worth spending much time over.

I got in the cab.

You'd think the fact that the runner was a Mexican would have tipped me off. It didn't, though. It was not until I saw the glimmer of starlight on the massive projectile before me that I knew I was in Arizona, and knew what the President had done for me.

A mixed squad of Pinkertons and our own plant protection men closed in on me and hustled me past the sentry-boxes, across the cleared land, up to the rocket itself. The OIC showed me the crescent he could make with thumb and forefinger and said: "You're safe now, Mr. Courtenay."

"But I don't *want* to go to Venus!" I said.

He laughed out loud.

Hurry up and wait; hurry up and wait. The long, dreary flight had been a stasis; everything at both ends of it had been too frantic with motion over which I had no control to permit thought. They gave me no chance to think here, either; I felt someone grabbing the seat of my pants, and I was hoisted inside. There I was dragged more than led to an acceleration hammock, strapped in and left.

The hammock swung and jolted, and twelve titans brooded on my chest. Good-by, Kathy; good-by, Schocken Tower. Like it or not, I was on my way to Venus.

But it wasn't good-by to Kathy.

It was she herself who came to unstrap me when the first blast was over.

I got out of the hammock and tottered weightlessly, rubbing my back. I opened my mouth to make a casual greeting. What came out was a squeaky, "Kathy!"

It wasn't a brilliant speech, but I didn't have time for a brilliant speech. Kathy's lips and my lips were occupied.

When we stopped for breath I said, "What alkaloids do *you* put into the product?", but it was wasted. She wanted to be kissed again. I kissed her.

It was hard work, standing up. Every time she moved we lurched against the rail or drifted off the floor entirely; only a standby jet was operating and we were otherwise beyond the limit of weight.

We sat down.

After a while, we talked.

I stretched and looked around me. "Lovely place you have here," I said. "Now that that's taken care of, I have something else on my mind. Questions: two of them." I told her what the questions were.

I explained about Runstead's lousing up San Diego and Venus project. And about Hester's murder.

"Oh, Mitch," she said. "Where do I begin? How'd you ever get to be star class?"

"Went to night school," I said. "I'm still listening."

"Well, you should be able to figure it out. Sure, we Consies wanted space travel. The human race needs Venus. It needs an unspoiled, unwrecked, unexploited, unlooted, un—"

"Oh," I said.

"—unpirated, undevastated—well, you see. Sure we wanted a ship to go to Venus. But we didn't want Fowler Schocken on Venus. Or Mitchell Courtenay, either. Not as long as Mitchell Courtenay was the kind of guy who would gut Venus for an extra megabuck's billing. There aren't too many planets around that the race can expand into, Mitch. We couldn't have Fowler Schocken's Venus Project succeed."

"Um," I said, digesting. "And Hester?"

Kathy shook her head. "You figure that one out," she said.

"You don't know the answer?"

"I do know the answer. It isn't hard."

I coaxed, but she wouldn't play. So I kissed her for a while again, until some interfering character with a ship's-officer rosette on his shoulder came grinning in. "Care to look at the stars, folks?" he asked, in a tourist-guide way that I detested. It didn't pay to pull rank on him, of course; ships' officers always act a cut above their class, and it would have been ungraceful, at least, to brace him for it. Besides—

Besides.

The thought stopped me for a moment: I was used to being star class by now. It wasn't going to be fun, being one of the boys. I gave my Consie theory a quick mental runthrough. No, there was nothing in it that indicated I would have

213

a show-dog's chance of being sirred and catered to any more.

Hello, Kathy. Good-by, Schocken Tower.

Anyway, we went up to the forward observation port. All the faces were strange to me.

There isn't a window to be found on the Moon ships; radar-eyed, GCA-tentacled, they sacrifice the esthetic but useless spectacle of the stars for the greater strength of steel. I had never seen the stars in space before.

Outside the port was white night. Brilliant stars shining against a background of star particles scattered over a dust of stars. There wasn't a breadth of space the size of my thumbnail where there was blackness; it was all light, all fiery pastels. A rim of fire around the side of the port showed the direction of the sun.

We turned away from the port. "Where's Matt Runstead?" I asked.

Kathy giggled. "Back in Schocken Tower, living on wake-up pills, trying to untangle the mess. *Somebody* had to stay behind, Mitch. Fortunately, Matt can vote your proxies. We didn't have much time to talk in Washington; he's going to have a lot of questions to ask, and nobody around with the answers."

I stared. "What in the world was Runstead doing in Washington?"

"Getting you off the spot, Mitch! After Jack O'Shea broke—"

"After *what?*"

"Oh, good Lord. Look, let's take it in order. O'Shea broke. He got drunk one night too often, and he couldn't find a clear spot in his arm for the needle, and he picked out the wrong girl to break apart in front of. They had him sewed up tight. All about you, and all about me, and the rocket, and everything."

"Who did?"

"Your great and good friend, B. J. Taunton." Kathy struck a match for her cigarette viciously. I could read her mind a little, too. Little Jack O'Shea, sixty pounds of jellied porcelain and melted wax, thirty-five inches of twisted guts and blubber. There had been times in the past weeks when I had not liked Jack. I canceled them all, paid in full, when I thought of that destructible tiny man in the hands of Taunton's anthropoids. "Taunton got it all, Mitch," Kathy said. "All that mattered, anyhow. If Runstead hadn't had a tap on Taunton's interrogation room we would have been had, right then. But Matt had time to get down to Washington and warn me and the President—oh, he's no Consie, the President, but he's a good man. He can't help being born into office. And—here we are."

The captain interrupted us. "Five minutes till we correct," he said. "Better get started back to your hammocks. The correction blasts may not be much—but you never know."

Kathy nodded and led me away. I plucked the cigarette from her lips, took a puff—and gave it back. "Why, Mitch!" she said.

"I'm reformed," I told her. "Uh—Kathy. One more question. It isn't a nice question."

She sighed. "The same as between you and Hester," she said.

I asked, "What was between Jack—uh?"

"You heard me. What was between Jack and me was the same as between you and Hester. All one way. Jack was in love with me, maybe. Some-

215

thing like that. I—wasn't." And torrentially: "Because I was too damn crazy mad in love with you!"

"Uh," I said. It seemed like the moment to reach out and kiss her again, but it must not have been because she pushed me away. I cracked my head against the corridor wall. "Ouch," I said.

"That's what you're so stupid about, curse you!" she was saying. "Jack wanted me, but I didn't want anyone but you, not ever. And you never troubled to figure it out—never knew how much I cared about you any more than you knew how much Hester cared about you. Poor Hester—who knew she could never have you. Good lord, Mitch, how blind can you be?"

"Hester in love with me?"

"Yes, damn it! Why else would she have committed suicide?" Kathy actually stamped her foot, and rose an inch above the floor as a result.

I rubbed my head. "Well," I said dazedly.

The sixty-second beeper went off. "Hammocks," said Kathy, and the tears in her eyes flooded out. I put my arm around her.

"This is a stinking undignified business," she said. "I have exactly one minute to kiss and make up, let you get over your question-and-answer period, intimate that I have a private cabin and there's two hammocks in it, and get us both fastened in.

I straightened up fast. "A minute is a long time, dear," I told her.

It didn't take that long.